T0209753

Shady Springs Ranch
Will It Be a Forever Home?

CONNIE SQUIERS

WESTBOW
PRESS®
A DIVISION OF THOMAS NELSON
& ZONDERVAN

WestBow Press books may be ordered through booksellers or by contacting:

WestBow Press
A Division of Thomas Nelson & Zondervan
1663 Liberty Drive
Bloomington, IN 47403
www.westbowpress.com
1 (866) 928-1240

ISBN: 978-1-9736-8065-9 (sc)
ISBN: 978-1-9736-8064-2 (hc)
ISBN: 978-1-9736-8066-6 (e)

Library of Congress Control Number: 2019919626

Print information available on the last page.

WestBow Press rev. date: 12/03/2019

With love to my sons,
Austin Stalnaker and Daniel Squiers and
to my friend, Rusty Kuester

Contents

CHAPTER 1
Brielle's New Foster Home

"Brielle, I want you to realize you're being given another chance to have a normal life with a loving foster family. The Kellingtons are an older couple who lost their daughter three years ago, and now they've decided they want to take in and love another child."

There was a long pause with no response.

"You can't run away again. Do you understand that? No one wants to take a chance on being responsible for a child who constantly runs away."

Another long pause with no response.

"People who take on this responsibility also invest their hearts when they open up to love another child." Vicki Stone shook her head as she watched the wipers swish the rain off her windshield. She wished she could see inside the head of the young girl sitting beside her.

Brielle looked out the window as the car sped toward her new home. *No, not home,* she thought, *a new place.* She already knew she'd hate where she was going and would run away again. Maybe next time she wouldn't be found.

When they pulled into the driveway, the Kellingtons came

out to greet them. They looked like they wanted to run toward the car, but they held each other back and slowed to a walk.

Brielle thought, *How lame.* She got out of the car and pulled her knapsack from the back seat. She didn't have much, but that meant there would be less to carry when she left. She wondered how long it would be before she grew tired of them and snuck out of the house late at night.

"Hi there, Brielle. Welcome to Wimberley, Texas. My name is Brenda Kellington, and this is my husband, Paul. Welcome to our home. We hope you'll like living here."

Vicki introduced herself to the Kellingtons and followed them up the porch steps. She then turned and looked out over the yard with its many pine trees and well-trimmed bushes. "Lovely place you have here. Brielle has always lived in the city, so this will be a good change for her." Then she turned around and entered the large and inviting log and stone home. She had always loved looking at houses, and this one was spectacular.

Brielle admired nothing and said nothing.

Once inside, Brenda turned and offered to get them iced tea and cookies if they were hungry. Vicki accepted the offer, but Brielle simply looked away and flopped down on the closest chair.

It was hard to make conversation with a person who refused to respond, but Vicki continued to talk as if she were getting answers. "Brielle, isn't this a lovely house? It's large and beautifully decorated. I think you'll like it here. I understand it's a working, cattle and horse ranch." There was a pause while she tried to think of something else to say. "Weren't those fences we saw on the way in pretty? And did you notice the horses in the pastures? You might like to go out to their stables later." She finally stopped trying to make conversation and quietly waited for the refreshments to be brought from the kitchen.

After the foster parent contract was signed, Vicki got up to leave. She leaned over and whispered to Brielle, "Remember what I said. This may be your last chance for a placement, and the Kellingtons seem to be a lovely couple. Give them and yourself a chance. This could be a wonderful place for you." She straightened up, turned, and walked toward the door, glancing back at the scowling young girl who had moved from the chair and was now sprawled out on the sofa. She silently offered up a prayer. *God, please give the Kellingtons the patience needed to break through Brielle's shell of indifference. Only You can turn this hateful and probably frightened young girl into someone loving and special. Help her see these people are being the hands and feet of Christ, offering to show her the way to a wonderful life of peace and contentment. Amen.*

After the door closed, Brenda turned to Brielle and offered her a hand. "Would you like to come upstairs with me to see your room?"

Brielle looked at her new foster mother's hand with disdain, then ignored it as she got up from the couch without help.

Brenda simply turned away and said, "Follow me."

Brielle followed but dragged her knapsack behind her, trying to make as much noise possible as they walked up the stairs.

Her room was beautiful. The walls were covered with a light wood paneling, and the floor was natural stone with thick rugs to take the chill off the feet on cold days. It even had an unusual wrought iron screen in front of the stone fireplace. She peered into the large bathroom, but said nothing. She'd never had a bathroom of her own, but she wasn't going to show them she was impressed. Besides, she wasn't going to stay anyway.

The four-poster bed was positioned so she could sit on her bed and look out the window at the Blanco River—not that it mattered. The beautiful quilt covering her bed was pieced together with muted fabrics, and the pillows lining the headboard were fluffed up, soft and full. When her new foster mother left, Brielle sat in a chair by the fireplace and stared into the fire that had been lit to warm her room. She refused to sit on the inviting bed. Tears filled her eyes when she imagined this home and family vanishing like all the others. She always left to avoid being tossed out, and she wondered how long it would be before she felt rejection again.

A tap on the door jolted her from those thoughts. She responded to the knock in a gruff voice, "What do you want?"

Brenda answered cheerily, "I just wanted to tell you we're eating in thirty minutes, so you'll have time for a quick shower."

She responded hatefully, "I don't want a shower."

"I'll come back and let you know when we're ready to eat."

"Suit yourself."

Brenda and Paul were making a salad and checking on the chicken roasting in the oven when Paul said, "Well, not a wonderful start, but we'll give her time. I just hope she allows herself to get to know us. It would be a shame if she cuts herself off from all the support and love we desperately want to give her."

Upstairs, a debate was going on. Brielle thought, *Should I stay up here and skip dinner to show them I don't care to be around them, or should I go down for dinner, eat, and run back up to my room?* Hunger won out. She could smell dinner cooking, and it had been quite a while since she'd had a home-cooked meal. Still wearing her old jacket, she slowly made her way downstairs, following the smell of food.

When she rounded the corner into the kitchen, Brenda said, "Hi! Glad you could join us."

Their cheerful attitude annoyed her, so she didn't respond. She would eat quickly and scoot back upstairs before they started asking her questions. There were always questions. She'd found that out.

As they were eating, Paul said, "Brielle, you're going to be living here, so if you'd like, you can call us Paul and Brenda instead of Mr. and Mrs. Kellington."

Brielle kept eating and didn't respond, but she thought, *Why should I call them Paul and Brenda? I'm going to be out of here soon anyway. I don't want them to think I'm getting friendly and fitting into their precious little family. If I keep calling them Mr. and Mrs. Kellington, they'll know I'm not going to let them sucker me into caring for them.*

Dinner was surprisingly pleasant. No questions were asked, and the only subject discussed was the horses they had on the ranch. As she was getting up to make her break, Paul said, "Brielle, since it's still light out, would you like to go down and see the horses?"

She hadn't expected that question. She shrugged and said, "Yeah, I guess." The talk of horses at the dinner table had made her curious, because she'd never even seen a horse up close. She didn't want to appear too eager, so she hung back as they walked toward the barn.

CHAPTER 2
The Rescue Horse

Brielle could hear the horses before she saw them. Evidently, neighs, snorts, banging, and stomping hooves were common sounds when they were being fed. Very few heads poked out of the stalls at feeding time because they were busy chomping and crunching on their food. It gave her a chance to look into the stalls without some old horse poking its head out and trying to bite her. When she finally peeked in one, she thought, *Oh my! They're huge!* She would've run out of the barn if she hadn't felt protected by a heavy mesh half door between her and the horse.

Mrs. Kellington looked over at her. "Well, what do you think? Are horses what you expected?"

Brielle shook her head no and then asked, "I know people ride horses, but why would horses let them? They could stomp a person in a heartbeat and kill them."

Brenda responded, "For some reason, horses seem to like people, at least people who are nice to them. Big dogs could easily slash people with their sharp teeth, but they don't unless they're mistreated. I believe God knew humans would need friends, so He made horses and dogs for us to use and enjoy." She chuckled. "Dogs and horses are *very* different from cats. It appears God made humans to serve cats."

That got a small smile out of Brielle because she *did* have experience with cats.

Brenda then asked, "Would you like for me to take this horse out so you can get a better look?"

Brielle backed up and stammered, "No, that's okay. I can see it from here."

When she got back to her room, she thought about the horses and how big they were. Brenda had petted each horse, and none had tried to bite her. In fact, when she gave them each a slice of apple, they didn't lunge and grab it from her. They simply nibbled with their lips and gently lifted it from the palm of her hand. Maybe there was something to God making horses to serve humans. She knew most dogs were like that too. They loved people to pet them unless they'd been abused and taught to hate. She would have to think about that. Then she began to wonder if people were also like that … rejecting people because they had been rejected … or because they expected to be rejected.

The Kellingtons saw very little of Brielle over the next few days. She ate with them, but stayed in her room the rest of the time, curled up in a wingback chair by the fireplace, reading the many books she found there. She thought this may have been their daughter's room and these were her books. She must have loved to read, too.

Occasionally, Brenda knocked on the door and peeked in, gratified to find Brielle with her nose in a book. *Good,* she thought. *She loves to read like my Tammy.* Those thoughts always brought a tear or two because she had many good memories of her daughter.

When Brielle had exhausted the supply of books in her room, she asked Mrs. Kellington if she could look in the downstairs library for more. She was told she could. When she left the library, she was asked who had taught her to love reading.

That was another question she hadn't expected, so she answered without thinking. "My mom loved to read before she started doing drugs. She would say it was a way to take a trip without leaving the farm." Brielle was afraid there would be more questions, so she quickly scurried upstairs and shut the door. Had she said too much? Why had she shared that her mother was a drug addict? She could have kicked herself. Giving out that kind of information would certainly bring more questions, and she hated questions.

A week later, Brielle was awakened by noise in the driveway. She looked out her window and saw Mr. Kellington talking to a man who had just driven in pulling a horse trailer. He motioned for the man to drive over to the barn and told him to wait for him there. Mrs. Kellington joined him, and they both trudged after the trailer. Brielle was curious and wondered what she was missing. She quickly threw on her clothes and joined the procession. When she got close to the barn, she hid behind a bush so she could see what was going on without being seen. It wouldn't be good to let them know she was curious about something going on at the ranch.

Mr. Kellington called out, "Mac, let the ramp down slowly and back her out. We don't want to scare her any more than she is already." A very scraggly, reddish-brown horse was backed down the ramp into the yard. It didn't look *anything* like the other horses on the ranch. This one was very skinny, with a matted coat, and looked exhausted.

Mrs. Kellington took the lead rope and went to the horse's head, giving her a pat. "It's okay, girl. Things will be better now." The horse nuzzled her and nickered softly.

Brielle wondered, *Why was that old horse brought here?* When her curiosity got the better of her, she stepped out from behind the bush. "Good morning. I heard someone pull up and saw everyone heading toward the barn. What's happening?"

Everyone looked up at the sound of her voice, surprised she was out of bed since it was only seven o'clock in the morning.

Mr. Kellington answered, "We have a new horse here at Shady Springs Ranch."

"*That's* the name of this ranch?" With a distasteful note in her voice, she asked, "Why did you name it *that*? It's a weird name for a ranch."

Paul smiled, eager to explain some of the history of his ranch. "Shady Springs Ranch has been in my family for many years, and it's never occurred to me to change the name. I imagine it was given that name because we have many springs on the property, and the water from our springs is not only cool but cold. And of course the trees make it shady."

"Why is it cold?"

Paul was happy to continue his explanation. "There's an artesian spring under our land that gives us spring water." He paused. "To better answer your question, it's so cold because the water in the artesian spring is stored in underwater caves located deep in the ground under Wimberley, where the heat from the earth's surface doesn't reach it."

All Brielle could say was, "Oh … if you say so." She quickly changed the subject with another question. "Why does that horse look so bad?" She had put her foot in it again.

Mrs. Kellington took no offense and answered the question with an explanation. "Several years ago, we heard about people who had lost their jobs or gotten sick and were unable to take care of their animals. There were cases where horses actually died from malnutrition because their owners couldn't feed them. We found several equine rescue organizations in the area that took these horses in when the owners were reported to animal control, so we contacted them to see how we could help. Believe it or not, many we have here at Shady Springs are rescue horses, which brings us to the horse brought in today. Several other horses found with this one had to be put down by the vet because they were too far gone, but this mare will probably make it with enough food and tender, loving care."

Brielle was amazed people actually cared about these dying horses, but she said nothing. She wondered what made people want to help animals ... and even kids. After lunch, she wandered in the direction of the stables, trying to act like the horses were not drawing her to them. She pitched a few pine cones in a nearby pond, then sat on a bench overlooking the creek that flowed into it. Finally, she stretched, then casually sauntered toward the horse barn.

Once inside, she peered in each stall, looking for the horse brought in earlier that day. It was behind the last door on the right. As she peeked over the door, she thought, *Poor thing.* It still looked a mess and didn't react when she clucked softly to get its attention. After several minutes, she slowly unlatched the stall door and made her way to the horse's head, watching to make sure it didn't turn and bite her. The horse didn't move, though she knew it had heard her. It just stared straight ahead into the dark corner of the stall. When she lightly touched its neck, its skin rippled as if trying to shake off a fly. The horse looked so pitiful it broke her heart. If only she had a bit of apple to offer. Surely it wouldn't bite if she gave it a treat. When she came out to the stable again, she'd have to remember to bring something horses liked to eat.

It looked like someone had brushed the mud from the horse's coat, but its fur was still dry and lifeless. When she moved closer, it turned its head toward her. Imagine her surprise when she saw warm, intelligent brown eyes looking at her. She didn't see fear or panic in them but curiosity. How could that be? This animal had been neglected and had almost died. She slowly held out her hand for it to sniff and was rewarded with a gentle puff of air.

She thought she'd be afraid if it made any sound at all, but she didn't even flinch. It was telling her she was accepted, and now they were friends.

Brielle thought a lot about the horse as she returned to the house. It occurred to her that she didn't even know if it was male or female. Earlier in the day, it had just been a poor, sad, ugly animal, and now they seemed to have a relationship ... a bond. She didn't understand how that happened, but she was sure it did.

CHAPTER 3
The Mistake

Brielle was quiet at supper that evening, because things seemed to be changing. She no longer hated the Kellingtons or wanted to leave, but she didn't want to talk about the change either. What would she say? That she suddenly felt something for a horse and she was beginning to learn nice things about the Kellingtons as well? How crazy was that? She would just keep quiet until she sorted it all out in her head. However, she did speak up and ask if the horse brought in that day was a male or female. They told her it was a mare—a female.

The next morning, Mr. Kellington ran in the house and yelled for his wife to call Dr. Rubin to come look at the new mare. Before Brielle could stop herself, she panicked and said, "What's wrong? What's wrong with the new horse? Is she going to be okay?" Paul and Brenda ran to the stable, and Brielle followed because she was worried. When they reached the barn, Brielle said, "She was fine yesterday afternoon. What could be wrong?"

They turned and asked her directly, "Were you out here yesterday afternoon?"

She responded defensively, "Yes. Why? I didn't do anything wrong."

Calmly, Paul asked, "Brielle, did you go in this horse's stall?"

"Yes, but was that wrong?"

Paul looked at his wife, then back at Brielle. "Did you make sure you latched the door when you left?"

She stammered, "I think so. It looked like it was closed."

He spoke to her gently. "Sweetheart, the door was unlatched ... in fact open when I went to the barn this morning. We think she got out of her stall and found the door to the feed room open because the lid to the grain bin had been nudged off on the floor."

Brielle responded hotly, "What are you trying to tell me?"

Dr. Rubin rushed into the barn before Paul could explain and interrupted. "Paul, let's see that sick horse of yours." After a short examination of the mare lying in the straw, he said, "I know you know that horses that have been starved should not be fed a lot of food, especially rich grain. The amount of fluids they drink should also be limited because they tend to swill down their water when they're thirsty. What did this mare eat after I left here yesterday?"

Paul rubbed his neck and answered, "I don't really know. We restricted her food, but I believe she accidentally got out of her stall and probably made it into the feed room."

The kneeling vet looked up briefly while running his hands along the mare's belly. "From what I can see, and from what you've told me, she probably has colic. Horses that have been starved often bolt down their food and water and are at risk of becoming colicky, but fortunately, this one doesn't look too bad right now. It's also possible she was so hungry the last place she lived that she grabbed at whatever grass she could and accidentally ate dirt and sand with it. That wouldn't have been good for her either. I recommend you make sure she has clean food and water, and remember, feed her regularly and don't try to plump her up with larger than normal meals. Her stomach just can't take it."

Brielle asked, "Is she going to be okay?"

When the vet stood up, he smiled and reassuringly patted her on the back. "I think so. I've given her a shot of something that will help her feel better, and I recommend she also be given a supplement in her food. Now let's get her up and start walking her around. Sometimes that helps expel the gas that's causing the pain."

Brielle started toward the house before Dr. Rubin even left the barn. She knew she was going to be yelled at—or worse—when the Kellingtons came inside. She didn't mean to hurt the horse, but she knew she was to blame because she didn't make sure the lock was fastened when she left the afternoon before.

Brielle heard them enter the house and began trembling when she heard them coming up the stairs. The door opened, and they both walked in. Brenda Kellington held out her arms and took her hands. "Oh, Brielle, I'm sure you feel terrible about not making sure the stall door was latched, but it was just a mistake … not done on purpose. In this house, we're not punished for our mistakes. We learn from them." She looked over at her husband and smiled. "Why don't we all go downstairs and have a big breakfast, because I'm starved."

Relief flooded over Brielle, and she responded, "If you don't mind, I'll be down in a minute." When they left, she fell on her bed, relieved the mare was going to be okay and shocked that the Kellingtons hadn't yelled at her for being so stupid. Tears silently slipped down her cheeks. Where did that emotion come from? She hadn't cried in years. Before going to the kitchen, she got up and quickly splashed water on her face, then combed her hair and put on clean clothes. When she first arrived at Shady Springs, it hadn't mattered if they liked her or not, because she knew she was leaving them anyway. Now, she wasn't so sure.

When Brielle walked in the kitchen, she looked different. Her thick auburn curls were pulled back in a pretty headband, and she looked clean and fresh. Even more surprising, she was smiling. Brenda and Paul looked at each other and shrugged. It was the first time they'd seen her look happy, and they were delighted.

That evening, the Kellingtons prayed, "Father, You tell us to praise You in all things. We know You didn't cause colic in our new horse, but You did give us a wonderful opportunity to show Brielle our love and grace. I don't think she expected to be forgiven for a mistake that caused that mare pain. When we saw the smile on her face after our little talk, we knew You were working Your magic in her heart. Thank You again for the opportunity to show her our love and to model the forgiveness You expect us to give others. Amen."

The next weekend, Mr. Kellington asked Brielle if she would like to take a ride with him to inspect fences on the property. She had been checking on the mare all week, and he thought it was time she saw something of the ranch.

She stammered, "But I don't know how to ride."

He replied, "Not a problem. I have a very gentle horse that will teach you all you need to know." And he was right.

The afternoon was beautiful, the sun was out, and there was a gentle breeze blowing from the south, making it a great day for a ride. After Brielle was on the horse, it simply followed Mr. Kellington's out to the corral. Though it looked like a long way to the ground, she wasn't afraid of falling because she had the saddle horn to steady her. She smiled and thought, *So this is what it feels like to ride a horse. Wouldn't those kids I left at the last place I lived be surprised to know I can ride a horse.*

As they rode, she finally asked a question. "Do you own all this land?"

"Yep. Most of it has been in my family for years. I've been fortunate enough to add a few acres to the place myself. As you can see, the land around Wimberley is gently rolling to hilly land.

What you may not know is Cypress Creek and the Blanco River run through it, and the land by our house is along the Blanco." She said, "Part of it is grassy, and some has trees. What kind of trees are these?" He replied, "We have lots of live oaks, red buds, and a smattering of dogwood." Paul then made a face. "And of course there are also cedars."

Brielle frowned and asked, "You don't like cedar trees?"

He replied, "Let's just say not many Texas ranchers can stand cedar trees. They invade the grasslands and are terrible water hogs." He looked over at her as they rode. "Did you know that a fifteen-foot cedar can use thirty-five gallons of water a day, which is nearly twice the amount used by an oak the same size? Cattle won't eat cedar, although I don't blame them for that. And what's worse, those nasty trees are everywhere, and it's almost impossible to get rid of them." He shook his head. "The unfortunate thing is many of the decent oaks on my property seem to be dying because the cedars drink up most of the water."

She asked another question. "How do you know so much about trees?"

He laughed. "It's been my hobby since I was a kid. I've always liked knowing what's growing around me."

Brielle asked yet another question. "Why do they call that tree you were talking about the dog tree?"

"Oh, you mean the *dogwood* tree." He raised an eyebrow and asked, "Are you sure you really want to hear all this?" Brielle nodded.

"Well, the dogwood tree originally came here from England. There, people used the bark to bathe mangy, smelly dogs—hence the name dog. After it was brought to America, the flowering dogwood was used by Native Americans to make scarlet dyes and an assortment of medicines. Although the pods are poisonous to humans, the colonists made tea from dogwood bark to reduce fevers and soothe colds. Today, the trees and their flowers are so pretty they're often used in landscape plantings." He glanced over at her. "Have I thoroughly bored you?"

Brielle shook her head no.

He suddenly stopped his horse and turned in his saddle. "Brielle, I want you to know how much Brenda and I love having you here with us. And don't think we haven't noticed how you've been pitching in and helping around the house and stable. You've become part of our team at Shady Springs, and I'm proud of you." Just as abruptly, he turned and kicked his horse into a trot, knowing Brielle's horse would follow.

CHAPTER 4
The New Horse's Name

When they arrived back at the ranch, Brielle noticed someone had let the new mare out to get fresh air and sunshine. Though she was still very skinny, she now held her head higher and neighed when they rode in the barn area. That was an improvement for sure. Up until now, she had shown little life except to shuffle over to her food bucket and eat. Brielle took the opportunity to get a better look at her because it had been so dark in the barn she hadn't been able to see her clearly. Her eyes swept across her coat. What was that color? She looked closer, and in the sunlight, it looked like copper thread shining among the brown fur. She'd heard the stable hands talk about another horse that color, saying it was a chestnut, so maybe this horse was too. She also noticed a little blackish brown in her mane and decided she liked the color.

Her gaze then moved toward the horse's head where she saw a thin, crooked blaze trailing down her face to her nose. *Character*, she thought. She thought the blaze gave her character, but those eyes are what captured her soul because they were trusting and friendly. She liked this mare despite how thin and pitiful her body still looked. Just as she was wondering why the Kellingtons hadn't given her a name, she heard a shout.

Brenda Kellington came running out to greet them as they

dismounted, and she was waving some papers. "Hey, guys! I have some great news for you, and it's about the new mare." She had their attention now. "Mr. Tucker, the former owner, has been very ill and is now in a long-term nursing facility, so I guess that's why he didn't take care of his horses. When his son was searching through his dad's records, he found some interesting documents concerning our mystery horse." She looked over at Brielle. "We haven't given her a name because we wanted to wait to see if we could find more information on her." She again studied the paperwork. "It says here her name is Cassidy, and she's registered with the American Quarter Horse Association, so she is a purebred quarter horse." She laughed as she glanced over at the horse. "Not that we can tell that by looking at her now."

Paul Kellington smiled broadly. "That's great news, honey. Not just that she is a purebred horse, but she finally has a name. I'll have a name plate made up for her stall this week." As an afterthought, he asked, "Do the papers say when she was born?"

Bewildered, Brielle interrupted. "What does that mean, that she's a purebred horse? I thought a horse was a horse."

"In this case, it means both Cassidy's parents were purebred quarter horses, which is very good, and eventually she should be a fine, and probably fast, horse … if we can get her fattened up."

Brenda interrupted and answered her husband's question. "Her registration papers say she's seven years old, and a note in the margin that says she's fifteen hands tall."

Brielle looked puzzled. "Fifteen hands?"

Paul explained, "That means she's sixty inches tall from the ground to her withers. Her withers is that little hump you see at the base of her neck. That's how they measure the height of horses, in hands. Each hand equals four inches."

Brenda noticed the confusion still on Brielle's face. "I'll explain it to you later, but right now it means she's a good size.

She's just right to be able move quickly and turn on a dime, which is a good trait for a cow horse. We just need to get her healthy."

Brielle didn't understand all of what she had just heard, but at least now she knew this mare had a name, and it seemed to fit her.

At dinner, Brenda asked, "How do you like the name Cassidy? It has a nice ring to it, doesn't it? I looked it up online, and it means either of two things—intelligent and clever or curly headed. I think she must be a pretty smart horse because she certainly isn't curly headed." They all laughed.

Brielle smiled. "Cassidy sounds fine to me. I'm just glad she now has a name. I'm tired of calling her *the* horse or *the* mare."

As the summer stretched into fall, Brielle looked back at all that happened since she'd arrived at the ranch. She found a new home she really liked and a horse she loved, and she'd learned to ride. She even attended church for the first time in her life.

Though Brielle knew she had to sit quietly in the church pew, there were times everyone stood and sang songs she liked but had never heard before. She had to admit she was a little confused by some of the words, like *there's power in the blood* and *I'll fly away, sweet Jesus.* She'd have to ask someone to explain those words to her because they didn't make much sense. She was also glad that Brenda had taken her to buy some nice clothes when she first arrived at the ranch, because she couldn't imagine wearing her old clothes to church. It wouldn't seem respectful, being sloppy in God's house.

CHAPTER 5
Becoming a Christian

A week before school started, Brenda called upstairs where she knew Brielle was reading. "Brielle, would you come in here a minute? I want to show you something."

Brielle was no longer afraid when the Kellingtons called her, but she couldn't imagine why she had been asked to come into the ranch office. She'd never been in there before.

"Come. Come sit down," Brenda said as she patted the chair next to her. "Have you ever worked with a computer before?"

Brielle shook her head no.

"Well, this is a great time to start. You'll be going into middle school next week, and I'm sure some kids in your classes will have computers, and at the very least, you should know how to work one."

Together they opened up the laptop on the desk in front of them. Brenda told her to watch as she started with a search on Goggle. She typed in quarter horse because she knew Brielle would find the subject interesting. The young girl was amazed to see an article on quarter horses come up on the screen—complete with pictures. She'd seen computers on television and knew they did amazing things, but this was unbelievable!

Next, Brenda suggested they type in B-r-i-e-l-l-e to see if her name had any special meaning. Sure enough, it did. One website is said it meant "God Is My Strength" and claimed its origin to be French and a short form of the name Gabrielle. Another site said it was a Hebrew name meaning "God Is My Might" and also "Heroine of God."

Brenda exclaimed, "Oh my, what a beautiful and powerful name you have, Brielle. I have always loved etymology, which is the study of the origin of words. I like to know how their meanings have changed throughout history. So does Paul. He told me he explained to you where the name dogwood came from, and I told you what the name Cassidy meant. I think it makes words more interesting, don't you? Can you think of another word we can look up?"

Brielle thought for a moment. "How about Sullivan, since that's my last name."

"Good choice. Okay." She instructed her to go to Google again and type in Sullivan and see what she could find. Brielle slowly pecked out S-u-l-l-i-v-a-n on the keyboard, and information appeared on the screen.

She leaned forward and read what it said, "It says Sullivan is an Irish name, and it means dark-eyed one." She looked up. "Pretty cool, except my eyes are green."

Brenda laughed. "And a bonny green they are, lass. By the way, *bonny* means beautiful in Ireland." She added, "My last name, Kellington, isn't Irish, but it's a small village in North Yorkshire, England. Maybe that village was named after our family."

All afternoon, they worked together on the computer. Brielle created an email address and then learned to send a message to Brenda and Paul. She also typed some gibberish and opened blank pages, then saved them in folders. Though she was pleased to be learning about the computer, she was more pleased to have

Brenda's time and attention. Grown-ups had never sat down with her to teach her anything.

When Brenda left to start dinner, Brielle offered to help her—another first for them both. While they were cooking together, Brenda told her she could have the laptop for school, explaining that many of the kids already used them in the classroom and it would help her take notes.

Brielle was astounded that someone would be that generous, but she only smiled and politely thanked her. She couldn't believe it. A computer of her own! Again, tears formed in her eyes, but she looked the other way so Brenda wouldn't notice.

Classes started, Brielle made new friends, and liked her teachers. She had always enjoyed school, at least when she was around to go. That was the only bad thing about running away: she missed going to school. She remembered classmates she'd known in the past who didn't like anything about school except recess. She thought the classes were great, but she especially liked going to the library. That's probably why she liked her computer so much. At the stroke of the keys, she could reach places she never dreamed she would see.

Sometimes Brielle had to pinch herself. She was living in a lovely home with nice people, there were lots of horses to ride, and she was getting an education. She wondered if this was what living in a *forever* family was like. If it was, she had missed out on a lot. Just maybe the Kellingtons would like her enough to keep her around. She brushed that thought from her mind, knowing it was only a dream. She was just a foster kid living with them for a while … but they sure were nice to her. Sometimes she wondered why.

One Saturday, when she was grooming Cassidy, her foster father stopped by and in a loud voice shouted, "It's time!"

Brielle was startled. "You scared me, and I almost dropped the brush."

He repeated, "It's time, Brie. Today's the day we ride Cassidy ... or try to anyway. We don't know that much about her training, so it might be a little rough."

"You're not kidding me, are you?"

"Nope," was the response. "I'm sure she isn't as fat and sassy as she once was, but I think she's strong enough to ride now. Put the rope on her and lead her down by the tack room. I have the saddle and bridle ready."

In a flash, Brielle did as she was told, and Cassidy patiently followed her outside. When being bridled, she readily accepted the bit, though she mouthed it because it was unfamiliar. The blanket and saddle came next with no problem. The mare puffed up a bit when Paul tightened the saddle's cinch, but he said that was normal. After he walked her around a minute or two, she relaxed. Then he tightened it again, knowing how embarrassing it would be to have the saddle slide off with him on it.

He led the mare out into the sun and said, "Well, here goes," as he mounted. Nothing happened. Cassidy stood still. He gathered the reins in his hand and urged her forward with a little cluck and nudged her with his heels. She walked until he pulled back on the reins. He looked down at Brielle and said, "Well, I guess she was used to being ridden. I really didn't know what to expect. Let's see if she neck reins." With one hand, he pulled both reins to the left, which put light pressure on the right side of on her neck. She followed his cue and turned left. He tried turning to the right with the same result. He commented, "This is great. She neck reins fine."

Brielle eagerly moved toward Cassidy, but Paul stopped her. "Brielle, I didn't mean *you* can ride her now. I need to give her a little more time under the saddle before turning her over to someone who just learned to ride a few months ago. She may suddenly get fed up with a rider and buck. You wouldn't like to be on her when she does that, would you?"

"You're right. Hey, can you make her go faster? I want to see her run."

In response, he leaned forward and kicked lightly. Immediately, Cassidy responded with a trot. Another little kick moved her up into a canter. She loped around the corral as if she had been ridden all her life. He hollered back to Brielle, "I'm going to do some figure eights and see if she changes leads. I'm not expecting it, but maybe she's had some training."

When he and Cassidy finished the figure eights in both directions, he returned to Brielle's side. "I didn't expect that. Her flying lead changes are as smooth as glass. This baby has had some schooling."

Always inquisitive, Brielle asked, "What's a flying lead change?"

He responded, "Let me explain, but I warn you, I may tell you more than you really want to know. Here goes. A lead refers to which set of legs, those on the left or the right, touch the ground before the legs on the other side. A lead *change* refers to the horse changing from one lead to the other. When a horse is using the correct lead, the inside front and hind legs reach farther forward than the outside legs." He stopped a moment and raised an eyebrow. "Too technical, or should I go on?" Brielle told him to tell her more.

"When a horse is using the correct lead, it's better balanced. If it's on the wrong lead, it may have a much harder time making turns. Making quick turns is especially critical for a working cow horse. A good flying lead change looks easy to anyone watching, because the horse won't speed up, slow down, or show its temper by hesitating or swishing its tail." He hesitated for a minute. "You still with me?" She nodded, so he continued. "Many cow horses change leads automatically so they can quickly turn and dodge cattle, but Cassidy has actually been taught, which we saw when she did the figure eights. That's a very good thing. I just wonder what her former life was like. My guess is she was shown at some point."

"You mean like at a horse competition or a rodeo?"

"Maybe." Paul looked down at Brielle. "Well, my time is up, and I don't think Cass is a threat to even you, so your turn."

Excited, Brielle squealed, "You mean it? I can ride her?"

"Yup, she's all yours. I'll give you a leg up, but you take it from there."

Brielle loved riding Cassidy, but she urged her into a trot only once the first day. She was afraid she'd fall off and wouldn't be allowed to ride her again for a while. Every few minutes, she patted the mare's neck and leaned over and gave her a hug. When it came time to dismount, she bent forward, put her arms around Cassidy's neck, and slid down her left side to the ground. She'd been so intent on her riding she hadn't noticed the Kellingtons smiling from the corral gate. They couldn't have been prouder had she been their own daughter.

CHAPTER 6
Change of Heart

Just before Christmas break, Brielle answered the phone, and it was Vicki Stone, the lady who had placed her with the Kellingtons. Just as she was telling Ms. Stone she would call Mrs. Kellington to the phone, she was interrupted. "Wait a minute, Brielle. I want to speak with you as well. How's it going? You're still there, and I haven't had any reports about you running away."

Brielle answered carefully, "It's been nice, and I like the Kellingtons."

"That's good because I heard they've enjoyed you as well. I'm glad to hear things are going smoothly. Do you still think about running away?"

Brielle blurted out, "Ms. Stone, you aren't calling to tell them you've found another home for me, are you?"

"Oh no, Brielle, nothing like that. I just want to make sure you and the Kellingtons are getting along. By the way, what's your favorite thing about living there?"

Without hesitation, she answered, "The horses are great … and the Kellingtons are too, but I really enjoy the horses."

Ms. Stone and Brenda talked briefly, but nothing was said about a change. Brielle had been holding her breath because she'd finally begun to put down roots at Shady Springs. It would hurt terribly to have to move away from the Kellingtons and this ranch.

That night in bed, Brielle talked to the Lord, thanking Him for bringing her to this place. She prayed before meals and in church, but prayer was really not a part of her life. Tonight, she felt overwhelmingly grateful for what she had and where she lived, because she was sure God had put her here. She spoke to Him as if He were in the room with her because at church that's what she was told she could do. They said God was everywhere, waiting for her to talk with Him.

She started her prayer with hesitation. *Father, I've been told You are all around me and You want to have a relationship with me, like a friend. It's so hard to believe the creator of the universe wants to listen to me personally. I've always assumed You were far too busy to listen to a young girl, especially one with not such a great past. I used to talk awful to everyone around me and never gave you a thought. Because I was miserable, I made them miserable too. I guess I was afraid to trust them because no one I'd ever known could be trusted. But I've come to trust You, and that's a big step for me. Please, Father, forgive all my sins because I know only You can. When I learned about You being the Son of God and dying on the cross for me, it brought tears to my eyes. I seem to be moved to tears a lot lately. I keep hearing about the Holy Spirit, and I wonder if that could be Him working in my heart. I hope so. Father, please bless the Kellingtons and of course Cassidy. I love You so much it hurts. Amen.* Julie didn't realize she had prayed the sinner's prayer and had become a Christian, entitled to everlasting life with Jesus.

Christmas was quite an experience at Shady Springs Ranch. They all decorated the tree together, and Brielle helped Paul hang lights outside. She paid special attention to a wonderful blue spruce that had been planted in the center of the circular driveway. The Kellingtons told her it had been planted their first

Christmas after moving to the ranch ten years ago, and it had grown at least ten feet since then. Their daughter, Tamera, had picked it out at the local plant nursery and had been very proud of it.

The day before Christmas, the house was full of holiday smells. Gingerbread, sugar, and mincemeat cookies had been baked, as well as pumpkin and apple pies. Brenda had generously taken the time to teach Brielle a few things she knew about baking.

Brielle commented, "You know, I'd never cooked or baked anything before you showed me. I'd never even made a salad. So, it's been wonderful to have a good cook around to show me what to do." She noticed a turkey in the fridge. "May I help with that too?"

Brenda was overcome with emotion and turned away. When she lost Tamera, she thought she would never experience the joys of motherhood again, which meant loving, guiding, raising, and sharing what she knew with a child. She sent up a short, silent prayer. *Thank You, Jesus, for bringing Brielle into our lives. She has filled a very empty space in our family and in our hearts. Amen.*

Since she was only a foster kid, Brielle didn't know what to expect on Christmas morning. She was not only overwhelmed with the presents she received, but the whole house was full of joy. The tree was beautifully decorated, Christmas music played, wonderful smells of turkey and dressing wafted throughout the house, and the Kellingtons took a few moments to pray before opening presents. They thanked God for His faithfulness to them, for the gift of baby Jesus so many years ago … and she was shocked to hear them thank God for her. When she lifted her head, she was speechless. The Kellingtons had actually said they were thankful for her.

Overwhelmed, she ran up to her room, leaving them wondering

what was wrong. A few minutes later, Brenda walked up the stairs and stood outside Brielle's room, not knowing whether to talk to her or to give her some time alone. She tapped lightly on the door, hoping to be invited in. When she heard sobs, she turned the doorknob and slowly opened the door. Brielle looked up from her bed with tears streaming down her face.

Brenda gently asked her, "What's the matter, sweetheart?"

Brielle responded between sobs and hiccups, "I didn't get you and Paul anything for Christmas because I couldn't get to a store and I didn't have any money anyway."

Brenda sat down on her bed and took her in her arms. "Brielle, don't you realize *you* are the gift? You have brought us more joy than you can imagine, and we've grown to love you." After a few minutes, she added, "I'm going to give you a few more minutes alone, but we would love for you to join us downstairs. We have one more present for you, and I think you're going to like it."

While the girls were upstairs, Paul hurried out to the stable to get the present. In a few minutes, he returned with Cassidy all decked out with a big red bow. He tied her to a post and scurried back inside just in time to see Brielle coming down the stairs. After he and Brielle joined Brenda in the kitchen, he suggested they go sit on the front porch and get some fresh air for a few minutes before dinner. When he opened the door to usher the ladies onto the porch, they heard a neigh. When Brie looked toward the sound, she saw Cassidy in the driveway all decorated like a fancy Christmas present.

Brielle turned to them and asked, "What's this?"

They answered in unison, "Merry Christmas, Brielle!"

She turned to them both, gave them a big hug, then ran down the porch steps to claim her present. "Are you teasing me? Are you really giving her to me?" Again, she broke down in tears, but this time she didn't run. Cassidy nuzzled her neck and nickered softly while Brielle hugged her, then stroked her neck.

She turned back to the two smiling faces on the porch. "Giving her to me is too much, but *please* don't take her back because I love her."

Paul said, "It seems we forgot that we have one more gift for you." With that, Brenda pulled a beautiful cream-colored Stetson from behind her back.

"A pretty cowgirl like you *must* have a suitable hat, especially when riding here in Texas."

Brielle let go of Cassidy and ran up the porch steps to hug them both again, saying, "Thank you, thank you, thank you. This is the best Christmas I've ever had."

CHAPTER 7
Weekend at Cypress Creek

In early January, Paul approached Brielle after she had completed her chores. "Hey, little girl, your mom and I have decided to take you to a special place we like, to go to get away from everything. Interested?"

Brielle had noticed the use of the word *mom* but didn't let Paul know she'd heard it.

She answered, "Sure. Where is it and can we ride there?"

Paul laughed. "You and that horse. You can't be away from her for a second. No, we can't take the horses, but it's a great place, and we're going to be there overnight."

Once the truck was packed and they headed out, Brenda commented, "It won't take us long to get there, and that's the beauty of it because we don't have to go very far. We know you'll love it as much as we do. By the way, it's right next to Cypress Creek, so we'll be able to hear the gurgling water from the porch."

Twenty minutes later, they pulled onto a dirt road marked only with a post with an iron horse head on top. About a quarter of a mile later, Brielle saw the house. It wasn't large or fancy, but a screened-in porch wrapped around all four sides. It could have used a coat of paint, and the boards on the porch steps needed replacing, but it had a warm, friendly look, and Brielle liked it.

As Paul unlocked the front door, he said with a flourish, "Welcome to our retreat." Once inside, Brenda started removing sheets from the furniture and handed them to Brielle, asking her to fold them and toss them in a nearby corner. Since it was only forty-five degrees inside the cabin, Paul opened the fireplace flue and went back outside to bring in some logs he had neatly stacked on the front porch. In no time, the fire was roaring, radiating warmth into the room.

Brielle commented, "What a cozy place this is, especially with the fire going. I can see why you like it here." She looked over at Paul. "Has this place always belonged to your family too?"

"No, but it might as well have been ours. My aunt Gracie had this place, and we used to have family get-togethers here. Sometimes we came out here in the cold months, but usually it was spring, summer, or fall, when we kids could sleep out on the porches. That way, we could hear Cypress Creek as we lay in our sleeping bags. When Aunt Gracie died, she left us this cabin because she knew we'd maintain it and always share it with the family … and we have. Though I don't have brothers or sisters, I have plenty of cousins, and most of them live around here. But tonight, this place is all ours."

Dinner was simple. There was no electricity at the cabin, so oil lanterns were lit, and the food was heated in a big iron pot that hung from a hook in the fireplace. With the hinged hook, they swung the pot over the hot coals to cook the meal, then swung it out when the food was hot and ready. Brielle thought it was just like the old days—at least like the old days she'd read about in books.

Three wingback chairs were pulled up to circle the fireplace, and they all put blankets over their knees, not to keep out the cold but to protect them from the direct heat of the roaring fire.

A portable radio played music in the background, but not loud enough to drown out conversation. The mood was warm and mellow. Paul started off with a prayer. *Father God, thank You for the delicious meal and thank You that we have a warm, quiet place to go when we want to be alone to talk and contemplate your Word. Guide our conversation and let this evening away from the world be peaceful and reflect the love we have for each other and for You. Amen.* Paul then reminisced. "There's so much I remember about this place and Shady Springs Ranch. Brenda, Tamera, and I used to come here on nights like this and sit around and talk like we're doing now." He also told of the many fun times he and his cousins had at their family reunions, then he became serious. "I guess the hardest time we had while staying here was when the police knocked on the door and told us our precious Tamera had been killed in a traffic accident. She was just twenty years old and starting her third year at Texas State University in San Marcos." He stopped for a minute to wipe a tear from his eye. "She could have gone to school at the University of Texas in Austin like we did, but she didn't want to live too far away. She said she'd rather commute so she could live at home and be around the horses. I often wonder if she'd still be alive if she'd gone to school in Austin, or if we hadn't told her to meet us here that night."

Brenda interrupted. "Paul, we've discussed this many times, and you know her being killed wasn't your fault. The three of us were happy with her choice. It just didn't work out the way we wanted."

She smiled and continued. "Let's talk about happier things that happened in our life, like how Paul and I met many years ago." She adjusted the blanket on her lap and began her story. "We were both students at the University of Texas and loved living in Austin. Paul was two years ahead of me in school and due to finish the next semester. Sure enough, he graduated, and right away he got a job offer with an oil company, but they wanted him to move to Dallas, so we had a decision to make."

Paul winked and interjected, "She made the right one. She stayed with me."

Brenda smiled at him and continued. "We had only known each other six months, but I was crazy in love with him. When he asked me to marry him and move to Dallas, I said yes, leaving all thoughts of school behind."

Paul continued the story. "We started out in Dallas, then moved to Houston, on to Wichita Falls, and finally back to Austin. That sums up our first eighteen years of marriage, always moving. When my dad died, my mom needed help on the ranch, and as an only child, I was obligated to help her. I tried commuting between Austin and Wimberley, but that became a real burden. Finally, we made the decision to retire from the oil business and move here to Shady Springs. Tammy was tired of moving, but when I offered to get her a horse if we moved to the ranch, she was more than willing to make one last move."

Brenda added, "Brielle, Tamera—we called her Tammy—was only thirteen at the time we moved here, which is only a year older than you are now. She took to this place like a duck to water, which made us happy."

Paul jumped in. "Unlike her mom, who had come to *love* living in big cities. I'm afraid Wimberley was a culture shock for Brenda, even though it was only about thirty miles from Austin and fifty miles from San Antonio."

She looked over at him and stuck out her tongue. "Don't be mean, Paul. I adjusted pretty quickly. Wimberley was just slower paced than I was used to. Besides, I was happy to see Tammy love it so much."

Brielle felt the lull in the conversation, but no one asked her questions. She finally said, "I guess it's my turn." She held her breath then jumped in. "You two have been so great about not prying into my life, so I think I owe you a little background. I was born in Amarillo, and I understand we lived there for a while, but my mom and her girlfriend thought it would be fun to move to the Austin area. Shortly after we settled in Austin, her roommate moved out, leaving mom with total responsibility for the rent, utilities, and food. It was downhill from there."

She paused. "Not long after that, she ended up bringing some very bad people into our home. I guess so they could help pay the bills. One person in particular hated me and slapped me around, sometimes even in front of my mom. Mom didn't like what our life had become, but what could she do? Eventually, she started doing drugs, and of course that took her attention away from me and used up most of whatever money we had." She looked over at Brenda, who now looked very distressed.

Brielle took another deep breath. "I finally ran away and was picked up by social services because I was begging on the streets. When they heard my history, they arrested my mom, and she was put in prison, where she is today. She was also charged with possession of narcotics with intent to distribute, because her live-in friends stored and sold drugs out of her apartment. Those charges were in addition to the child endangerment and child neglect charges placed against her. I guess that's about it and why she won't be out anytime soon."

Quickly, she added, "Oh, I almost forgot. I ran away from the other foster homes because they asked me lots of questions and were *so* sure I was just like my mother. I heard them say that many times. Besides, I didn't get along with most of the kids in those places. They made fun of me because my mom was in prison, but I often wondered why *they* were in foster care if their homes were so great."

Brenda reached over and reassuringly patted her arm. "You know that means nothing to us, except that we know you were hurt, which makes us sad. You're no longer that runaway foster child, and we see your heart. You may not know this, but we specifically asked social services not to tell us your background, though of course they were required to tell us your mom was in prison."

Paul suddenly jumped up to change the subject. "Hey, what do you say we play some cards." He looked at Brielle. "If you don't know any card games, we can teach you some fun ones."

Later that night, Brenda and Paul hugged her good night and tucked her in a cozy feather bed in the loft above the living room. Before they went downstairs, Brielle asked in a timid voice, "Do you mind if I call you Mama K and Papa K ... because it's easier." What she really meant was it made her feel more like she was part of a family.

They answered, "Of course not, sweetheart. Good night."

That night, before Brenda and Paul went to sleep, they hugged each other and cried about the terrible life Brielle had before reaching them at Shady Springs and then came tears of joy because Brie had just taken a big step closer, making them feel more like a family.

CHAPTER 8
Meeting Mr. Tucker

After school one mild winter day, Paul asked Brielle if she would like to see just what her horse might have been trained to do. He hadn't been on Cassidy since the first time he had ridden her, but he was sure Brielle was curious too. They saddled Cass and took her to the corral. Once he mounted and warmed her up, he began asking her to do more than just walk, trot, and canter. He leaned forward, gave her firm kick, and she broke into a gallop. When they reached the other end of the corral, he stopped her suddenly by pulling the reins tight. She leaned her back on her haunches, and they slid to a stop. *Beautiful*, he thought. Again, he tried the figure eights, but at a greater speed than the first time he had ridden her. The result was a same. Cassidy changed leads as if it was the most natural thing in the world.

Two ranch hands heard the commotion in the corral and went out to see what was going on. When they saw their boss riding Cassidy, they called out, "Way to go, Mr. K." It was a real treat to see those two in action because watching them was more like a performance. They edged over to where Brielle was standing and said, "That's quite a horse you have."

Earlier, Paul had set up two barrels to see if they looked familiar to Cassidy. When prompted, she leapt forward and took the turns around the barrels fast, without touching them at all. It was evident that at some point she'd been trained to barrel race. After again racing to the other end of the corral, he pulled her to a fast stop then asked her to back up, which she did without hesitation.

He rode back to the gate for a few minutes to let Cassidy rest. "Brielle, I doubt she can do some of the things I'm going to ask of her now, but we'll see." Then he guided her to the center of the corral, reached down, and patted her neck, saying, "Here we go, girl." He kicked her into a gallop, making large circles, keeping them as perfectly round as he could. He then started to slow and patted her again. "So far, so good, Cassidy." He gradually decreased her speed to a slow lope, reining her in ever smaller circles. Then he reversed direction. No matter which direction or what speed she was going, she changed leads, making the transition between the large and the much smaller circles look effortless. When Paul was done, all he could say was, "Wow!"

Next, he tried a roll back maneuver, which involved Cassidy coming to a complete halt, stopping squarely on her haunches, then rocking back on her hocks and making a 180-degree change of direction. She performed beautifully. Under his breath, he again said, "Wow!"

Brielle shouted to him, "Why would Cassidy need to do that?"

He replied, "Think about it. A good cow horse needs to be nimble, change directions quickly, stop on a dime, then sprint after a loose cow. You see, as the cow turns, the horse draws back over its hocks, then turns with the cow. A horse and rider must work as a team to anticipate the cow's next move and keep it from turning back into the herd."

"What other things should a horse do in a competition?"

Paul replied, "I've already shown you she can stop and turn, but let's see if she can do a 360-degree spin in place. *If* she can do it, her hind legs will remain in one place, and she will rotate 360 degrees, using her forelegs to propel her around in a complete circle. That's useful when she's working a cow because it means she can sit back on her rear end and move her front end, front legs extended, to follow a cow. That's called a sweep. I'm willing to bet she can rotate the other way as well." Sure enough, she changed direction and completed the spin perfectly.

Brielle commented with pride, "Cassidy can do just about everything, can't she?"

"She sure can. Maybe next week we can take her into a pasture where we have cows and find out if she knows how to cut— meaning separate specific cows from the herd."

"She's so smart I'm sure she can. That'll be fun to watch."

Paul smiled. "Not to mention it'll be fun to ride a horse that can really work cows."

Brielle and Paul were jubilant as they entered the house, prompting Brenda to ask, "What put those big grins on your faces?" They told her, and she congratulated them on the great day they'd had.

Chapter 9
Brielle Forgives Her Mother

A few days later, while they were cleaning up the kitchen, Brielle suddenly asked Brenda, "You believe in forgiveness, don't you?

Brenda was so surprised at the question she almost dropping the bowl she was drying, "Of course I do."

"The pastor talked about it last week, so I've been thinking I might forgive my mother for leaving me. What do you think? Should I forgive her?"

Brenda wiped her hands dry and turned to Brielle. "Well, God calls on us to forgive everyone, so I think it would be a wonderful thing to do. Do you want to write to her?"

"I thought it would be a good idea. That way, I can put down exactly what I want to say instead of … you know … talking to her on the phone and accidently saying something that might make her feel worse than she already does."

Brenda took Brielle's hand and led her over to sit at the kitchen table. "Do you know which prison she's in?"

"No, not really, but I think Ms. Stone would know. I was thinking I might call her tomorrow, if it's okay with you."

"Of course it's all right with me. I think it's a wonderful idea. And, Brielle, I'm proud of you for wanting to forgive your mom."

Brielle didn't know it, but Brenda and Paul had been praying for that very thing. They knew that people who don't forgive those who have hurt them remain victims, and the other person isn't even aware of the pain they continue to cause. When someone gets very sad or feels an emotional stab in their heart when they think of someone who hurt them, it means they are still linked to that person in a negative way. They were certain if Brielle would forgive her mom, it would free her spirit.

After Brielle was given the address she requested from Ms. Stone, she wrote her mother a short note telling her she still loved her and hoped she was doing well. After signing it *Love, Brielle*, she added *Mom, you made poor choices that hurt me a lot, but I forgive you*. Then she added her phone number.

A week went by, and Brielle had no response to her letter.

One Saturday morning, Paul called out, "Hey, Brielle, we have another nice day, so we should take advantage of it. How about we saddle up and ride out to see the cattle?"

Brie was excited and replied, "Only if you ride Cassidy, because I don't know what she'll do when she sees cows. She might shy away or lurch off after them and leave me in the dirt."

Paul didn't object because he was *very* eager to see Cassidy in action and find out if she had been trained as a cow horse. From what he had seen so far, she probably had been.

When they got to the pasture, Brielle looked around in amazement. "Look at the beautiful bluebonnets. They're everywhere!" Then she yelled over to Paul when she saw the cattle, "There they are. I didn't know you had so many cows. And look! It seems like they're floating in an ocean of blue flowers." She then turned her attention back to Paul. "I'll stay back here, and you and Cassidy go do your thing."

She didn't have to tell him twice. He started toward the cattle at a lope and picked out the calf he wanted to cut from the herd. When the cows saw the horse and rider coming toward them, they started to move, then to run. Paul reined Cassidy toward a calf at the edge of the herd he wanted separated out. It started running away, then doubled back when it became confused. The horse immediately crouched down, ready to pivot whichever way it ran. The little rascal ran one way, until he was blocked, then tried the other direction. Cass had him under control and was forcing him away from the herd. To show Brielle her horse was doing the cutting and not him, Paul loosened the reins and tried to anticipate her movements so he wouldn't fall off when she turned. In no time, Cassidy had penned the cow in a corner until she was signaled to let him go.

Paul trotted over to where Brielle was waiting. "This is some cow horse you have here, missy. Now let's try a deep cut and get one from the center of the herd. That's more difficult."

He looked over the herd and pointed. "See that little heifer over there? The one with the white face and a splotch of red fur on her head? That's the one we want." He gave Cassidy a pat on the neck and a kick, and they were off, with the herd scattering out before them. He guided her toward the heifer, and that was all he had to do. Once Cassidy realized which cow was the target, she overtook it, put her head down, and worked it out of the herd like she had the other one. Once again, Paul let the reins go slack and stayed with her for the ride. He touched the reins only to let Cass know where he wanted her to take the heifer they'd cut out.

The horse was a joy to ride, but at the same time, he wished he could be *watching* her work the cattle, because he knew it was a beautiful sight. It was obvious Cassidy missed pitting herself against a cow, trying to second-guess which way it would turn. It was a game to her, and she loved it.

When Paul headed over to the gate to talk with Brielle again, Cassidy kept looking back, wanting to play some more. When they got close enough, Brielle reached out and hugged her horse's neck. "You are such a special girl, Cass. I watched you out there, and you showed those silly old cows who was boss." She looked up at Paul with a smile. "So I guess she did okay."

He laughed. "Yeah, she did okay, and if you twist my arm hard enough, I might agree to ride her again."

Brielle was not afraid to ride her horse back to the barn, but she was not ready to ride her into a herd of cattle. Cassidy might take over and do her own thing. What if she misjudged which way her horse was going to pivot and fell off? She knew she'd have to practice riding a while longer before doing something crazy like that on Cass.

On the way back to the ranch, Brielle said, "I saw two donkeys mixed in with your cattle. Why were they there?"

Paul turned to her. "It was very observant of you to see those donkeys, and the answer is going to amaze you. Some ranchers add them to their herds because donkeys and mules are very aggressive and attack predators, like coyotes, for example. It probably makes the cattle feel more secure, but more importantly, it makes me as a rancher feel better because I know they're guarding my cows."

Brielle commented, "I didn't expect you to say that."

He laughed. "Another animal that protects herds is the llama."

She looked at him in disbelief. "You've got to be kidding me. A llama?"

He looked over at her. "Google it or look it up on YouTube. It's fun to watch them protect herds of sheep and cows. Unfortunately, they'll also chase dogs away they don't know. Check it out when we get home." She smiled at him, and he knew she'd do just that.

Brielle and Paul entered the house with the same grins they had on their faces a few weeks before. Brenda smiled and commented, "I take it Cassidy liked the cows."

Paul answered, "Do ya think? She *loved* the cows. I'm not sure what that horse did where she lived before, but she wasn't left in a field to eat grass all day. That's for sure."

The phone rang, and Paul answered it. Brielle heard only half the conversation, but she was sure it was about a possible horse rescue. Once he got off the phone, he said, "An animal rescue organization just told me there are a couple of horses needing help in Seguin and asked me if I'd take a look. I told them yes and was wondering if maybe you and I could take a side trip to Lockhart, where they picked up Cassidy. We could ask around a little and maybe find someone who knows more about Cass. We might even visit Mr. Tucker, the former owner, and see what he remembers about his horse. I'm going to call his son to see if there might be other paperwork in his dad's house that could give us more information."

They hooked up the trailer and decided to visit Lockhart first so any horses they picked up in Sequin wouldn't have to be in the trailer so long. Paul said, "I called Mr. Tucker's son Greg, the one who lives in Lockhart, and he agreed to meet us at his dad's place. He explained that his father was in such poor health that he had to put him in a nursing home to get him the care he needed. He also encouraged us to stop by the facility to pay his dad a visit, so it should be an interesting afternoon."

When they arrived in Lockhart, Greg Tucker was waiting for them at the ranch. Once they were inside the old fifties-style rancher, they started looking around. Immediately, Brielle noticed a large bulletin board covered with faded newspaper clippings and ribbons. "Look here! I wonder if Cassidy won any of these." They both scanned the board, looking for her name. Sure enough, she'd won ribbons in many western events.

Excitedly, Brielle again pointed to the board. "Papa K, look at this one. It says she was a barrel racer. And this one says she won blue ribbons in reining and cutting competitions."

Paul looked over at Greg and asked if it was okay if he took the clippings and ribbons back to the ranch. The response was, "Sure. I don't think Dad will need these now."

Curious, Brielle asked him, "Did you used to ride Cassidy?"

He responded, "Nah, I was never into horses, but my older brother was before he moved to New York state. He and my dad trained our horses, but Randy's the one who rode in the competitions."

As they were getting ready to leave, Greg pointed to a stack of old magazines in the corner. "I don't know if these old *American Quarter Horse Journals* interest you, but my dad had a subscription, and he and Randy pored over them every month. He said they contained great articles, and I think your horse was mentioned in them a time or two."

Immediately, Paul said, "We'll take them all."

Once everything was loaded in the truck, they headed to see Mr. Tucker. When they found the facility where he now lived and finally located his room, he was gazing out the window. Paul tapped on the door. "Mr. Tucker, may we talk with you for a few minutes?" Then he introduced himself and Brielle.

The frail man slowly turned his wheelchair around and stared at them. Greg Tucker was right; though his dad wasn't an old man, he looked very sick. He growled, "What do you want?"

Paul started hesitantly. "We understand you had a horse named Cassidy, and we hope you can tell us a little bit about her because she's living at our ranch now."

His scowling face softened, showing a hint of a smile. "What do you want to know?"

Brielle said, "Mr. Tucker, we've noticed that Cassidy is a very well-trained horse. Did you train her?"

He got a faraway look in his eyes, as if remembering. "Yes, me and my boy Randy trained her. What a special horse she was.

Quick on her feet and quick to learn too." He turned his attention back to his two visitors. "Why are you here?"

Brielle stepped forward and took his limp hand. "Cassidy is my horse now, and I want to thank you for all the work you and your son put into her. I've come to love her very much."

Mr. Tucker looked away, then looked back at her with tears in his eyes. "I felt so bad when I could no longer take care of her, and I am glad she's in a place where she's loved. She was my very favorite horse, and believe me, I've had many horses."

Paul asked, "Mr. Tucker, did you ever use her as a cow horse?"

He responded with a weak smile, "Oh yes. My Cassidy was the best I'd ever seen at working my cows. We used to have lots of land and cattle, but it got to be too much for me after Randy left, so I sold almost everything I had. Couldn't bear to get rid all of my horses though. They were my friends."

After he was given another shot for his pain, he started nodding off and mumbling. Brielle thought she heard him say, "Take care of my Cassidy," before he drifted off to sleep, still sitting in his wheelchair.

When they got back in the truck, Brielle was thoughtful. "It's good to know Cass was always loved. That's probably why she is such a sweet, gentle horse. I'll love her until the day I die."

Picking up the horses in Seguin was accomplished quickly. Paul noticed they were quite thin but in much better shape than Cassidy had been when they first saw her. He knew they'd recover quickly and fit right into the herd at Shady Springs Ranch.

CHAPTER 10
Letter from Mom

Spring was short, and the summer heat bore down without mercy on Central Texas. If it hadn't been for the trees at Shady Springs Ranch, it would have been sizzling hot. Brenda came downstairs and asked Brielle if she'd like to go somewhere special to cool off. The answer was an immediate yes!

She declared, "Then let's grab Paul and our bathing suits and head for the Blue Hole." She looked over at Brielle. "It's not that the Blanco River and springs we have here aren't cool, but sometimes it's just good to get away from the ranch. Besides, it's way too hot to ride today." Brielle agreed.

Once in the truck, she asked, "What is this Blue Hole you're talking about and where is it?"

Paul answered in his usual informative way, "Believe it or not, it's a wonderful swimming hole surrounded by 126 acres of natural forest and native grasses right smack dab in the center of Wimberley. The water there is cool—chilly really, which makes it refreshing on days like this. Lots of people in Wimberley like to go there to beat the heat."

After two hours of splashing and cooling off at the Blue Hole, Paul suggested they visit Jacob's Well. Again, Brielle asked him to tell her about it. "Well, it's really a cave about 120 feet long, and its mouth, which opens up in the bed of Cypress Creek, is twelve feet in diameter. Thirty feet of the cave is straight down, so it's quite a deep hole. This cave is different from others because water from the Trinity Aquifer feeds a powerful underground artesian spring that gushes from its mouth. Water from Jacob's Well feeds the rivers and creeks around here, as well as the Edwards Aquifer, which provides most of the water in this part of Texas. As you can imagine, water from this spring even makes it down to the Gulf of Mexico."

He added, "When we get there, notice that the water coming up from the cave ripples to the surface, but I understand it used to be so powerful it pushed water up about six feet in the air, kind of like a big geyser. It must have been fun to feel that big gusher underneath you."

Brielle was curious and asked, "Why doesn't it shoot up like that now?"

Paul was more than happy to answer. "Central Texas has more people than it used to, so we use more water, making the water level in the aquifer low sometimes. It doesn't help when there are droughts, or periods where it doesn't rain enough.. The lower the water levels, the lower the water pressure. That's why we don't see those six-foot gushers anymore."

Intrigued, she asked, "Is it dangerous to swim in the well?"

"It's no more dangerous than other swimming holes, unless you're scuba diving and try to explore the caves deep inside it. There have been people killed doing that."

When they arrived at Jacob's Well, Brielle carefully slipped into the cool water, holding onto the rocks surrounding the well. She thought the dark hole looked like it would suck her down under the water, but in reality, the water was gushing up and out instead.

That night, Brenda and Paul came in to kiss Brielle good night. "Well," Brenda said, "did you have a good day?"

They both smiled, and Paul added, "A day without riding. Imagine that. It doesn't happen around here very often."

Brielle replied, "It was fun. I've never been to a swimming hole before, and those were great. Maybe we can go back again sometime this summer."

Paul smiled. "I bet we can. Good night, sweetheart, and sweet dreams."

Before she drifted off to sleep, she remembered something she had seen at Shady Springs the first day she arrived. There was a sign on the front door that read *Love Spoken Here*. She didn't understand what it meant at the time, but she did now. The Kellingtons were kind, loving people, and everyone who met them knew love was in their hearts … for horses, other people, and young girls without hope.

Brielle had expected her mother to respond to her letter right away, but that was not to be. After the third week of waiting, she no longer expected a return letter and went on with her life at the ranch. Exactly one month after she had written and mailed her note, Brielle received a letter from her mom. Before opening it, she ran to Brenda and asked her to stay in the room with her as she read. She was afraid of what it might say. Maybe her mom would tell her not to bother writing again. She opened it up with trembling hands and read aloud.

My dearest Brielle.,

I apologize for not getting back with you sooner, but I was transferred to another prison, and it took a while for my mail to follow.

I was surprised to hear from you because I thought you probably hated me for how badly I let you down. I'm glad to know you've become a Christian because I'm a Christian now, too. I'm also glad you've found a good foster home and people to care for you.

There's a wonderful group that comes here to talk with us. The Kairos Prison Ministry blesses us because they are not judgmental, but just love us and tell us Jesus does, too. Many of us are now saved because of that group. Since you are a Christian now, no matter what happens, we will see each other again in heaven. Sometimes I can hardly wait.

You may not think I think of you, but I think of you both and wish I had done better with my life so I could be with you.

Write when you can, and I will always answer. It will always be a blessing to hear from you.

Love,
Mom
XXXOOO

Brielle's eyes opened wide as she read the last two paragraphs a second time. She looked up at Brenda and asked with tears in her eyes, "Mama K, what did she mean? She said I think of you both." Her panicked voice was shrill. "What did that mean? I'm an only child. I would know if she had another baby, wouldn't I?"

Brenda took the letter from Brielle's shaking hands to read it for herself. "It definitely sounds like she said she had two children." She put her arms around her. "Brielle, don't panic. Write her back tonight and ask her why she said both. She probably just made a mistake. Let's not worry about it until we know the whole story."

A week later, she had her answer.

Dear Brielle,

I'm sorry to have shocked you with my letter, but I didn't know at the time I was arrested that I was pregnant. I was certain the foster care people would have told you I had a baby while in prison.

You have a sister, and I want you to find her. Lillian is almost six years old now. That's what I named her anyway. They may have changed her name though. Her birthday is actually two days after yours, April 22.

Please contact the people who put you in foster care and ask them why you were never told about your sister. I was hoping she would be placed with you.

I would write more, except there's nothing here to write about except that I have Bible study twice a week. I hope you are still learning about Jesus too.

Again, I love you both, and I hope you meet your sister soon.

Love,
Mom

When Brielle first read the letter, she was excited about having a sister. Then she was mad she'd not been told about her. She wanted to call Ms. Stone right away and ask her why no one had told her. She had the right to know!

Brenda said, "Brielle, why don't we be happy that you have a sister instead of being mad at the system. You can't reach Ms. Stone until Monday anyway. I think we should go out to dinner and celebrate." She looked over at Brielle with a sly grin on her face. "Just maybe we can talk Papa K into taking us to Austin …

to *Matt's el Rancho* for Mexican food. I know you always like eating there. Then maybe we can drive over to Sixth Street and walk around to see what's going on."

After Paul agreed to take them to Austin that afternoon, Brielle was in a much better mood. Nothing she could say now would change the fact that she'd only just learned about her sister, so she might as well celebrate like Mama K said.

CHAPTER 11
Brielle Meets Her Sister

When they reached Matt's, Brielle focused on the menu. She loved steak fajitas, but she also liked chilies relleno.

Mama K urged her to get the fajitas and said she would order a plate of chilies relleno and share one with her. Brie thought that was a great idea. When they prayed before dinner, they thanked God not only for the food, but also for finding out that Brielle had a sister.

Later, Brie commented, "You know, you were right, Mama K. Finding out about Lillian, or whatever her name is now, is a real blessing. If I hadn't chosen to forgive my mom, I never would have known. I can hardly wait to call Ms. Stone on Monday to find out where she's living. Maybe she can come for a visit."

When they were in the truck after leaving Matt's, Paul asked, "Does anyone feel like walking down Sixth Street? We might hear some good bands down there."

Brielle and Brenda answered yes at the same time.

They drove to Sixth Street, a famous Austin landmark located between Congress Avenue and I-35. Brielle had heard it was the heart of Austin's entertainment scene, but she'd never been there. As they walked along Sixth Street, she saw old buildings that now housed numerous bars, lots of live entertainment, tattoo parlors, art galleries, and casual cafes to fancy restaurants. Music could be heard everywhere—everything from jazz, to rock and roll, to country. The sounds poured out of the doors, inviting people to come in.

"Papa K, can we go inside to listen?"

He replied regretfully, "No, sweetheart. Most of the music is coming out of these bars, and you aren't old enough to legally drink in Texas, so we'll have to sit outside. But don't worry. There's plenty to see out here. All kinds of people walk down this street, and you'll have a front-row seat. We can't stay long anyway, but I wanted you to see the Sixth Street you've always heard about."

After an hour of crowd watching, they made their way back to the truck. It was almost sunset, so Paul suggested they go down to the Congress Avenue Bridge to see the Mexican free-tailed bats. As they watched the bats swarm out, Paul said, "The other day I read that from 750,000 to 1.5 million bats come out from under that bridge each evening they are in Austin, and at the peak of the bat-watching season, which is from March to November, they cover the countryside in search of food. The article estimated that on their nightly flights, the bats consume from ten thousand to thirty thousand pounds of insects." He added, "That's a lot of bugs and mosquitos, isn't it?"

Brielle was amazed and pointed to the people in canoes floating around the bridge watching the bats. She looked up at Paul. "This is a *really* big deal, isn't it?"

"Yes, it is. It's estimated that more than a hundred thousand people a year visit the bridge to witness the bat flight, making millions of tourist dollars a year for Austin. Apparently, it's the largest urban bat colony in the world."

Once all the bats left the bridge, the three of them made their way back to the truck with Brielle rattling on about all they had seen that day. The Kellingtons had taken her to Austin so she would think of something besides her sister, and they had succeeded.

At the breakfast table on Monday morning, Brielle patiently waited to contact Ms. Stone about finding her sister. At eight o'clock on the dot, she called and was glad to hear a familiar voice on the other end of the line. She blurted out, "I got a letter from my mother, and she said I have a sister. Why didn't you tell me? You were supposed to tell me."

"Hold on there, Brielle. You said your mom told you that you have a sister?"

"Yes, and I want to know where she is."

Confused, Ms. Stone responded, "This is the first I've heard about your having a sister. I'll call you right back after I check the records."

"Sure." Then she hung up the phone. Ten minutes later, the phone rang. "Hello."

"Brielle, this is Ms. Stone. I just looked in your file, and there is no mention of a sister. If we had known, we would have placed her in a foster home with you. If you'll be patient, I'm going to find out why we weren't notified, because somehow a mistake was made. I'll call you back."

This time, it was almost two hours before Brielle and Brenda received the call. "I tracked down a file that showed your mom *did* have a baby, but it took a long time to find your sister's placement records. Evidently, she was a crack baby, which means she was born addicted to drugs and had to be placed with foster parents who care for such infants. Once they knew she'd be okay, they were told there was a family member who wanted to raise her. I don't know why all this information wasn't put in your records since you are related to her, but I do know she lives in Texas."

Concerned, Brielle asked, "Who took her? Who was the family member that wanted her?"

Ms. Stone looked over the records again, then answered, "Apparently her grandmother wanted her."

Brielle responded with anger in her voice, "I don't know of any grandmother."

Mama K touched her arm. "Calm down, Brielle, and let Ms. Stone talk." Brenda then asked her for more information about her sister.

"Mrs. Kellington, since the mother had no known relatives, the father's mother was notified and told Social Services she wanted custody of Lillian."

"So her name is still Lillian? We weren't sure what her name would be. Where does this grandmother live?"

Ms. Stone answered, "Lillian lives with her grandmother in San Antonio, which is not that far from Wimberley."

When Brielle heard the name of the city, she interrupted. "But how do I reach her? Do you have a phone number I can call?"

"Yes, I do, and I've already contacted the grandmother and let her know you'll be calling them. I hope that was okay."

As soon as they got off the phone with Ms. Stone, Brielle made the call. She was excited but wasn't sure what she'd say. She practiced saying, "Hi. I'm your sister. You don't know me, but we have the same mother." When someone answered, she simply said, "I'm Brielle Sullivan. May I speak with Lillian?" As soon as her sister's name was out of her mouth, she choked up. Would Lillian like having a sister? Would she even want to see her? She hoped so.

The woman on the other end said, "One moment please," and was gone.

A moment later, a small, hesitant voice was on the phone. "This is Lillian. Who are you?"

Brielle couldn't believe she was hearing her sister's voice for the first time. "Lillian, you may not have been told I would be calling, but I'm your sister."

Lillian responded in wonder, "Really? Are you *really* my sister?"

Brielle laughed. "I guess so. I just found out I had a sister, and that's why I haven't called until now."

They talked briefly, then Lillian's grandmother came on the line. "I guess we'd better set up a time to get you and your sister together." Brielle listened but left it to Brenda to work out the details of the meeting.

Three days later, Brielle and the Kellingtons drove to New Braunfels, where it had been decided the girls should meet for the first time. Brenda had searched the internet, and together she and Lillian's grandmother had come upon a little restaurant named *Oregano's* on State Highway 46. Pizza was always popular with kids, and by meeting midafternoon, there wouldn't be a crowd, so they could talk comfortably.

Brielle was nervous as they drove toward New Braunfels, but not nearly as nervous as Lillian. She whined, "Litta, when will we be there? I want to meet my sister!"

Her grandmother answered, "Lillian, calm down. We'll be there soon."

She responded in panic, "What if I don't like her, or what if she doesn't like me? What if—?"

"Hush, my *chiquita*. Don't worry. You will love each other because you are sisters from the same mother."

When Brielle asked the same questions, Mama K answered her, "What's not to like? Anyone would love you, especially a sister."

The Kellingtons and Brielle arrived at *Oregano's* first but didn't get out of the car. A few minutes later, another car drove up and parked next to them.

When Lillian got out, she closed the door softly behind her and stood still, waiting for her grandmother to come around and take her hand. When Brielle looked over at her sister, she saw a little girl who was very unsure of herself. Brielle could definitely relate to that feeling. She had met many new foster parents, and she'd always felt the same way, not knowing how they would act or if they would even like her. This made her heart melt.

She got out of the car, stepped forward, and reached out with both hands. "You must be my sister, Lillian. I'm Brielle, and I could hardly wait to meet you."

Relief flooded through Lillian, and tears filled her eyes. In a small voice, she said, "Me too," then took the offered hands. Before she knew it, Brielle had wrapped her in a big bear hug of acceptance. Lilly was no longer afraid.

Once inside the restaurant, Lillian's grandmother nodded at Brielle and her foster mother, saying, "My name is Benita Santos, and this, of course, is my granddaughter, Lillian." They all sat down together, with the sisters sitting next to each other. Though twelve, Brielle was short for her age. She had auburn hair, pale white skin, big blue eyes, and a smattering of freckles across her nose. Lillian was five years old, very petite with coal-black hair, warm brown eyes, and light olive skin. Though they were different, it was obvious they were related because they both had a mass of curly hair, the same turned-up nose, and identical smiles—big, wide, and warm.

Lillian leaned over to her sister and whispered, "I was so afraid you wouldn't like me."

Brielle whispered back, "I wondered what I would do if you hated me." Their fears had been so much alike they laughed.

Lillian's grandmother smiled and asked, "What are you girls laughing about?"

"Oh, nothing," they said in unison.

To make conversation, Brenda told Lillian's grandmother, "I like to study names, and I think Benita means blessed in Spanish, and Santos comes from the word saint." Benita just smiled and nodded.

Lillian turned to her sister and suddenly said, "You don't look very much like me."

Brielle answered, "That's probably because we had different fathers. Was your dad from San Antonio?"

She answered, "Yes. Was yours?"

Brielle's face clouded for a second. "I don't know where he was from, and I never met him to ask."

Lillian smiled. "I never met mine either. That's one way we're alike." She continued matter-of-factly, "My daddy's dead. Is yours?"

Brielle responded, "I'm not sure, but I've never heard from him, so I guess he might as well be. I don't think about it."

Once the girls knew they liked each other, they exchanged phone numbers and promised to call each other regularly.

CHAPTER 12
Visit to San Antonio

School had started again, so the only time they could get together was on the weekends. Lillian had an idea. "Brielle, why don't you ask your mom — I mean your foster mom — to bring you to San Antonio this weekend, and we can go to the zoo or down on the River Walk."

"The River Walk? What's that?"

Lillian responded in amazement, "You mean you've never heard of the River Walk in San Antonio?"

"I'm afraid not. The Kellingtons have taken me quite a few places, but I've never been to San Antonio. It's a big city isn't it?"

"Big is not the word! It's *huge*! Please, please ask the Kellingtons if we can meet there, and I'll show you both the zoo and the River Walk."

Brielle knew she was seven years older than Lillian, but she was her *sister*, and she wanted to be around her. She'd never had anything like a sister—not even a good friend. Going to see those places with her sister would be fun.

The Kellingtons agreed to take Brielle to San Antonio to meet with Lilly and her grandmother, knowing she would enjoy both the zoo and the River Walk. That afternoon, Brenda called

Lillian's grandmother and worked out the details. They would make a day of it.

The day chosen turned out to be one of those beautiful Indian summer days where the temperature was much warmer than normal for fall. The Kellingtons picked up Lillian and her grandmother at their apartment then headed for the zoo. When they got there, Brielle looked around in amazement. She'd never see anything like it. Not only were there birds and animals but fish and flowers as well—all in one beautiful place.

When Brielle saw and heard a peacock squawk, she jumped. "What is *that*?" It set her sister to giggling.

"That's a peacock. They make that awful sound you heard, but they sure are pretty, aren't they?" She paused a moment, then said, "I bet I know something you don't know."

"About peacocks?"

Lillian nodded and answered smugly, "Yup. Only boy peacocks have those pretty feathers. I guess that's to make the girl peacocks like them. The girl peacocks look very plain."

Brielle responded, "I didn't know that, but I read that's true for lots of birds, like cardinals and mallard ducks, for instance."

The girls sped off to find the monkeys, leaving Brenda, Paul, and Benita behind. Brenda looked at the other two and commented as they girls rushed away, "Looks like we must assume the zoo's a safe place for the kids. Would you like to find a seat, talk, and watch people? I love to do that."

Two hours later, the sisters found the adults still sitting in the same place. The girls' tongues were hanging out from thirst, and their hands were out begging for money so they could get something to eat.

Paul gave them each enough money for a drink but told them they had to wait to buy something to eat when they got to the

River Walk. Pleased, they scurried off to find a place that sold soft drinks.

It was easy to find the River Walk because Grandma Benita was in the car giving them directions. When they got there, the girls insisted they were starved, so finding a good place to eat was first on their list of things to do. Paul spoke up and pointed as they got within sight of the San Antonio River. "That looks like a nice place. The food must be good too, because there are people lined up to get in. While we're waiting to be seated inside, we can sit outside under umbrellas and watch people go up and down the river in those riverboats."

Brielle read the sign aloud, "Casa Rio." She turned to Lillian and asked what it meant.

She responded, "It means river house."

Paul then asked the girls, "What do you want to eat?"

They both answered, "Mexican food," which was not a surprise.

Lillian could not read the menu since she was only five, so when her sister asked her if she would like to order a combination, she nodded enthusiastically, then asked, "What's a combination?"

They all laughed while Brielle explained, "The combination plate has a chicken enchilada, one tamale, chili con carne, and Mexican rice. Does that sound okay?"

"That sounds good. I was a little worried about ordering a combination because I didn't know what it was." Her eyes twinkled with glee as she continued, "I thought it might be a little tough and hard to chew, but if you ordered it, I would've given it a try." When they all looked surprised, she chuckled, hoping they didn't really think she thought a combination was an animal of some kind.

Brielle and the Kellingtons looked at one another and smiled, thinking Lillian had a good sense of humor and fit in nicely with their family.

When the food came, the girls wolfed it down and then began looking around to see where they might want to go next. "Whoa, girls, you need to sit here for a few minutes until we're done. We aren't as young and energetic as you two. I bet you're looking at the riverboats, aren't you? That might be a good next step so we can see exactly what the River Walk has to offer."

Sure enough, twenty minutes later, all five of them were on a riverboat headed down the river. Lillian had been on the river twice, but it was Brielle's first time. She was amazed at how beautiful everything looked, especially the bridges over the water. She commented, "I saw pictures of these riverboats on the menu at Casa Rio, and they looked so pretty at night."

Paul commented, "We'll have to come down here some evening, maybe a little closer to Christmas when they have the Christmas decorations up as well." Brielle was all for that.

She noticed faint strains of music up ahead and asked about it.

Lillian's grandmother said, "That's mariachi music—folk music from Mexico. It's a cultural thing for us who live in San Antonio, especially if we came from Mexico."

Brielle exclaimed, "Wow! It sure is happy music."

As the riverboat wound around and looped under bridges and passed inviting stores and restaurants, Brielle admired the wonderful stone paths that ran along either side of the river. This looked like a fairyland to a girl from the wrong side of town, and she found it enchanting.

Before the Kellingtons dropped Lillian and her grandmother off at their apartment, Lilly asked, "Brielle, when can I see where *you* live?"

Embarrassed, her grandmother scolded her. "Lillian, that's not a polite question at all. Apologize to the Kellingtons."

Glumly, she said, "I'm sorry."

Brielle knew it hadn't been a polite question, but what could you expect from a five-year-old, especially one who is your sister?

Paul Kellington said, "Lillian, we've already been thinking we should ask you and your grandmother to come for a visit. How about next weekend?"

She smiled and clapped her hands in anticipation.

When the day was over, the girls were exhausted. After dropping Mrs. Santos and Lilly off at their apartment, they headed back to Wimberley. By that time, Brielle was so tired she lay down in the back seat of the car and fell asleep until they pulled in the driveway at Shady Springs. She forced herself to get out of the car and made it up to her bedroom without even checking on Cassidy.

One week later, Benita's old car pulled into the driveway and stopped next to the house. When they got out, Lillian immediately ran up to the steps to find Brielle, but her grandmother stood still for a minute, looking at the fine house. She was almost embarrassed to think they had seen her apartment building when they had come to pick them up. But when Brenda saw her standing there, she ran down the steps and gave her a big hug of welcome and then said with a very American accent, "Buenos días mi amiga. Did I pronounce that right?" That made Benita feel better.

She laughed. "Yes, you pronounced it right, and I'm glad to be your friend." She looked around at the yard before they entered the house and commented, "Es muy hermoso aquí," which meant "It is very beautiful here."

"Gracias. I'm glad you like it, and I'm *very* glad you and Lilly have come for a visit."

As they entered the house, they could hear the girls laughing upstairs in Brielle's bedroom, and Benita said warmly, "I'm so glad they like each other. It is such a blessing for them both." As they headed toward the kitchen, Brenda noticed the older woman was wobbly and holding on to furniture as she walked.

Concerned, she asked, "Benita, are you okay? Sit here, and I'll get you a cool drink of water."

Lilly's grandmother responded, "Thank you so much. It would taste very good right now."

When Brenda sat down with her in the kitchen, she said, "This would be a great time to get acquainted. How long have you been in the United States?"

"We came here from Mexico over thirty years ago and settled in San Antonio, so it seems like I've always lived here. My two girls were born in Mexico, but my boy, Lillian's father, was born in the United States." She smiled. "He is … I mean he *was* a US citizen."

Brenda hesitated but asked, "So your son is no longer living?"

Benita shook her head sadly. "No, he's gone, and I will tell you the story. My Carlos was a good boy but got mixed up with bad friends and drugs. He wanted to make money quick and started selling them but was caught and put in prison."

Brenda put her hand on Benita's arm. "Oh, I'm so sorry, and please know that you don't have to tell me all this. It must be painful to talk about."

"Yes, it's painful, but you should know." She gazed out the kitchen window. "He moved from San Antonio to Austin and found a place to stay with Brielle and her mother. Before long, she and my Carlos were arrested, convicted, and put in prison for a very long time. After Anne was sent to prison, she found out she was pregnant, then had a baby. It was only after Lillian was born that Carlos was told he was a father. The poor baby was what they call a crack baby because her mother was on drugs while she was pregnant. I wasn't called to take her until Lillian was no longer addicted. At first, I didn't believe she was my grandchild, because Carlos hadn't told me about the baby, but they ran tests, and he really was the father." Benita had tears in her eyes. "After I brought her home, I took her to see her dad. That was first and only time he saw her … and the last time I saw him. He was killed by another prisoner during a fight. It broke my heart, but I was glad he got to see his daughter at least once." She looked over at Brenda. "He cried like a baby you know. I think he was happy and sad at the same time."

Brenda hesitated, but she wanted to know more. "Did you ever contact Anne and tell her you had her baby?"

"No, I never did. I just wanted to take Lillian home and not have any more to do with prisons."

Brenda asked, "Do you think she knows you have her? Social services told me they told her, but she didn't write. Maybe she thought it would hurt too much to not be able to hold or raise her."

Brenda told her that Brielle's mom had never contacted Brielle either, but she and her mother had recently begun writing. "That's how she found out she had a sister. Anne mentioned it briefly in her first letter, which made Brielle want to meet her. You know the rest of the story."

When they heard the kids clomping down the stairs, they both started to stand up, but Benita fell back in her chair with a heavy thump.

Brenda was worried. "Benita, are you sure you're okay? You're sweating. Would you like a cool cloth for your forehead?"

"Yes, that would be nice. I've not been well, and I need to take my medicine shortly, so may I bother you for another glass of water?"

"Yes, of course."

When the girls burst into the room, Lillian was excited. "Brielle is going to take me out to look at the horses. It's okay, isn't it, Mrs. Kellington?"

"Sure, that's fine. When you see Paul, please tell him his lunch will be ready in thirty minutes. So will yours, so make it a short visit."

Brielle assured her they wouldn't be long.

Once they left, Brenda glanced over at Benita, who had her head resting on her arms now folded on the table. "You don't look well at all. Would you like to go lie down for a bit while the girls are outside?"

Benita looked up slowly. "You are so kind, and yes, I would love to lie down for a little while."

Brielle and Lillian raced for the stable, passing Paul on the way, telling him about lunch as they ran by. When they got to the barn, Lillian noticed a dog near the door gnawing at a flea on his front paw. She stooped down by the dog and petted him. "Aww, such a nice dog. It makes me miss my dog."

Surprised, Brielle asked her, "You have a dog?"

Lillian answered, "Yes, I have a dog, and I love him. My grandmother hasn't been feeling well, so my aunt's been taking care of him."

"What kind of dog is he?"

Lillian looked up and explained, "I don't know because we got him at the pound, but he's very friendly."

"What's his name?"

Lillian got a big smile on her face and said proudly, "His name is Ready."

Surprised, Brielle said, "You've got to be kidding. Why would you name him Ready?"

Lillian explained, "Well, when we got him, he was ready to eat, ready to go for a walk, ready to play, and ready to fetch a ball. We just hoped he would be ready to growl if someone tried to get in the apartment. That's why we named him Ready."

Brielle rolled her eyes and looked away, saying, "Whatever. It makes sense to me."

As they started walking down the aisle between the stalls, the horses began poking their heads out to see who was coming. Lillian said, "They won't bite me, will they?"

Very matter-of-factly, Brielle answered, "Of course they will." When she looked over at her sister, whose eyes were as big as saucers.

With fear, Lilly whispered, "They *will* bite me?"

Brielle laughed. "No, silly goose. They won't bite you. You just have to learn how to make friends with them. I grabbed a few carrots from the fridge before we came out here so you can feed one to Cassidy."

"Cassidy is your horse, right?"

"That's right. She's the one in the end stall that just neighed when we came in the barn. She wants to make sure we see her and give her a special treat."

Amazed, Lilly asked, "You mean she knows you?"

Brielle responded with pride, "Yup, she knows me. I'm her best friend. We saved her, you know. Animal Rescue found her almost starved to death and brought her here to Shady Springs Ranch. She was very skinny when she got here, but you'll see. She's a big, healthy girl now."

When they got down to Cassidy's stall, Brielle showed her sister how to hold the carrot so Cass wouldn't accidently nibble on her finger. Lillian was surprised the horse didn't grab for the carrot right away but sniffed and blew on her hand. It felt good, but she wasn't expecting the horse to smell and blow on her first. Brielle explained that her horse just wanted to check her out before taking the treat.

Immediately after Cassidy took the carrot from her, Lilly quickly pulled back her hand, causing the mare to toss her head and back up.

Brielle said, "You've got to be calm around horses because they don't like quick movements. If you're in the wrong place when she shies away like that, she could step on you. You wouldn't like that, would you?"

Lillian shook her head no.

When they were almost done petting the other horses in the barn, Brielle heard the dinner bell clang and shouted, "It's time to eat! I'll race you to the house."

Brielle could have easily beaten her sister, but she let her win. However, she didn't expect Lillian to go in the house bragging about it. She just shook her head, reminding herself that her sister was just a little girl.

Though it was a little chilly outside, when lunch was over, Paul asked, "Who wants to ride a horse?"

Lillian jumped up and down. "I do! I do!"

"Well, let's get back outside and down to the barn, but I don't want you to run because it upsets the horses."

Lillian headed for the barn, trying not to run by taking long, slow steps. Brielle just watched and shook her head.

When they got there, Paul asked Brielle, "Which would be a good horse for Lillian to ride today? Thunder?"

Brielle knew he was teasing because Thunder was not an easy horse to ride. He always tried to run away with whoever was on his back. "Nope, not this time," she responded. "How about Honey?"

He smiled at her. "Honey it is. I'll go saddle her up for Lillian. You go get Cassidy ready because you two are riding together. Today you'll stay in the big corral because I want you to show your sister the basics of riding. Can you do that?"

"Sure. Come on, Lilly. Let's get Honey out of her stall and watch Paul saddle her. Remember what I said: you've got to be quiet around the horses, especially when they're being saddled. You can't sneak up on them, or they might act up."

Lillian watched from a safe distance, and when she was asked to come and get on the horse, she was very nervous. The one they had chosen for her to ride was so *big*. What if it ran away or did something to make her fall off? It was a long way to the ground. Brielle took her hand and pulled her toward Honey. "Don't be afraid. When I lift you up, put your left foot in this stirrup. And see the big knob up here on the saddle? That's called the saddle horn. Grab it with your left hand, stand up in the stirrup where you put your foot, then fling your other leg over so you'll be sitting on top of her. Don't worry. She's not going anywhere because I'll hold onto her bridle. And don't worry about the stirrups. I'll adjust them when you get settled."

Lillian was very brave and did as she was told. "I'm on top of a horse! I'm really riding a horse! I never, ever thought I would get to ride one!"

Brielle scolded her, "Lillian, you've got to calm down. Now take these reins in your hands, but don't pull them too tight. The reins are how you'll guide your horse. If you pull on them or hold them too tightly, Honey won't go anywhere."

Lillian countered, "But I don't want her to go anywhere."

Brielle laughed. "Not right now you don't, but you will. Stay right here until I get on Cassidy."

The two of them rode slowly around the corral with Brielle shouting instructions. "Loosen up on those reins. Back straight. Act like you're not afraid of your horse." Then she praised her. "That's a girl. I think you've got it." Paul stood by the fence just in case Lilly felt she needed his help.

When they got off the horses, Lillian walked funny, just as Brielle expected she would. She asked her big sister, "Are you sore after you ride?"

"Nah, not now, but I was when I first started. You'll get used to it."

Brielle took the saddle off Honey while Lillian held the reins and patted the horse. "Brielle, Honey is a nice horse and pretty too. What color is she?"

Brielle answered, "She's what we call a sorrel because she has a reddish-brown coat and her mane and tail are a little lighter." Then she asked, "Did you like riding today?"

"I did and wait until I tell Litta I rode a horse."

Brielle looked surprised. "Who is Litta? I thought your grandmother's name was Benita."

Lillian laughed. "Litta is short for *abuelita,* which is little grandmother in Spanish."

Brielle just shrugged and started walking toward the house. It was time for a cool glass of lemonade and maybe a snack.

Mama K and Lillian's grandmother were waiting for them. The girls had been riding for more than two hours, so Benita had been able to take a long nap and looked much more rested now.

"Lillian, are you ready to go home?"

Lilly whined, "Not really."

Brenda said, "That's okay, Benita. We'll be eating dinner in about an hour, and we'd love to have you two join us."

"Thank you so much. You've already done so much for us today. We'll leave after we help clean up the dinner dishes."

Lillian cheered, "Yay! Thank you! Thank you!" Then she asked, "What's for dinner?"

CHAPTER 13
Lillian Visits Shady Springs Ranch

The weeks passed, and it was almost Christmas. Lillian asked her sister, "What are we going to do for Christmas?"

Brielle knew exactly what she wanted to do. "I'd like to go back to the River Walk and see the Christmas lights."

Papa K said, "That sounds like a great idea. Let's plan on it."

The afternoon they were returning to San Antonio came, and the Kellingtons and Brielle picked up Lillian and her grandmother at their apartment. Of course, Lillian was excited.

The River Walk was as lovely as Brielle expected, but instead of heading out to explore, the first thing they did was sit down because Benita seemed to be in distress. Concerned, Brenda asked, "Are you okay? You don't look well."

Benita responded, "I just need to sit down for a minute. You and the girls can leave me here, and you walk around for a while. I'll be fine."

Paul said, "Brenda, why don't you stay with Benita, and I'll take the girls down to where the riverboats turn around and come back. They need to work off some of their excess energy."

Right after they left, Benita grabbed Brenda's hand. "I need to talk to you. As you can see, I'm not well, and I will be going in the hospital next week for tests. I hate to ask you this, but could you possibly keep Lillian for a while … just until I feel better and get back on my feet?"

Brenda moved closer and put her arm around her shoulders. "Of course we'll take her. You know we've grown to love Lilly, and Brielle is crazy about having a little sister."

As they continued to talk, Brenda looked more closely at the older woman sitting next to her. She noticed that Benita's clothes seemed to hang loosely on her, and her skin looked pasty and gray. She took a Kleenex from her purse and wiped away sweat that had formed on the old woman's brow, even though the temperature outside was cool.

She asked, "How long have you been feeling this way?"

Benita answered, "A few months now. Sometimes I feel okay, but I often feel sick and hot like I do now. That's why I'm having some tests run. I guess when you get to be my age, things go wrong with your body. I just worry what is to become of my Lillian. I would ask my daughters to keep her, but I know they have kids of their own and not much money to spend on an extra mouth to feed."

Brenda patted her hand and reassured her, "We can keep Lillian as long as necessary, but in order to get her in school in Wimberley, we'll need to get legal documents giving us temporary custody of her. Is that okay with you?"

Benita started to cry. "I'm old and not well. I've been very worried about what will become of my granddaughter."

"Let's just enjoy this evening and deal with what we have to do later. When we take you home tonight, you can pack some of her clothes, and we'll take her back to Wimberley with us. I have plenty of room at the house, and Lillian seems to like it there. Remember, you'll be able to talk with her whenever you want, and we'll give her back when you're feeling better."

That evening, the Kellingtons told Lilly she could either call them Paul and Brenda or Mama and Papa K since she would be living with them for a while.

Christmas day came, and everyone packed in the car and drove to San Antonio to pick up Benita. Lilly found it hard to sit still because it had been almost a week since she'd seen her abuelita, and that visit had been in the hospital. She hoped she'd get well, but she knew that might not happen.

When they returned to Wimberley with Benita, the girls piled out of the car, but Lilly's grandmother was much slower since she now had to use a walker. The steps were a problem until Paul scooped her up and deposited her inside the house before she could even object. Once she was settled on the couch, she looked around at the room the girls had decorated the week before. The ceiling was high, so they had a lovely twelve-foot tree fully trimmed with twinkling lights, many multicolored glass balls, and garland.

Benita said breathlessly, "It's quite lovely, girls. I've never seen a prettier tree. Once I catch my breath, I may get up and take a closer look." She never did catch her breath or move from the couch. She sat quietly in the living room while those around her moved to the kitchen to put the final touches on dinner. It had been a tiring day, and all she really wanted to do was lie down for a while, but she knew she couldn't nap now. It was Christmas, and leaving the festivities would be rude.

She heard Lilly call from the other room, "It's time, Abuelita. Come see the beautiful table and help us eat all this food."

Benita struggled to her feet but did not move until her granddaughter came in to get her. Once at the table, she sat quietly, listening to the hum of conversation and the carols playing faintly in the background.

Brenda finally asked her, "Benita, aren't you hungry tonight? You've hardly touched a thing." She gently offered, "How about some of those Mexican tamales you brought? It was so nice of you and your daughters to share them with us. You make them every year, I bet."

Benita answered slowly, "Yes, it's a tradition among my people. Tamales are a part of Christmas and a nice way for the women to get together to cook something for their families." Though her explanation about tamales was not long, everyone could see it exhausted her to talk.

Brenda was concerned. "I think a short nap before we open the presents would do you some good. We'll all clean up in here and call you when we're done."

"Oh, thank you. That would be nice."

After Benita was settled in a downstairs bedroom with her door closed, Brenda spoke softly to the others. "She doesn't look well, and if she doesn't look better after her nap, we should probably take her back to San Antonio … maybe even call her doctor and have him meet her at the hospital." She had considered taking her to the hospital in Wimberley, but she knew Benita would resist that. Besides, she would be more comfortable in her own home, with her own doctor, and if necessary, going to her own hospital. Brenda knew she'd feel the same way.

Rather than waking Benita after cleaning up the kitchen, they went in beside the tree and quietly opened presents. The gaily wrapped gifts were appreciated, but they didn't keep anyone from thinking about the sick woman in the spare room. When they finally heard her stirring, they led her out into the living room, asked her how she felt, then handed her gifts. She hadn't expected there to be gifts for her. For Lillian, yes, because she was a child, but not for her. She wiped tears from her eyes and let everyone hug her.

When Paul mentioned taking her back to San Antonio, she was ready to go. Before they got in the car, she drew Brenda aside and asked, "Can you keep Lillian a little while longer? It would be easier that way."

She gave the older woman a hug and said, "Of course we can. She's always welcome here."

Instead of taking her to her apartment, they called one of her daughters, explained the situation, then dropped her off at their house.

As the days got longer and warmer, Lilly's grandmother improved slightly, but she was no longer able to live in her apartment alone and now lived with her oldest daughter, Maria. Lillian was able to visit her grandmother once a week, but she didn't believe she would ever live with her again. The Kellingtons had taken her into their house temporarily as a foster child, but Lilly was afraid social services would soon find another place for her to live. She prayed every day that wouldn't happen. She liked where she was now ... with her sister.

CHAPTER 14
Driving Snowflake

Late one morning, when the girls were out by the stables, Lilly noticed and pointed to a pony in a nearby pasture.

"Brielle, what's that pretty little horse's name?"

"That's Snowflake." Then she challenged her younger sister. "I bet you can't guess why they named her that."

Lilly hesitantly ventured a guess. "Because she's white?"

"Bingo! Ding-ding-ding, you guessed it! Because she's white!"

Curious, Lillian asked, "Why is she at Shady Springs? Was she a rescue horse too?"

Brielle explained, "No, but there *is* a story behind her coming here." She had Lillian's full attention now. "When Tammy, the Kellington's daughter who died, was still alive, she had a horse named Snap. I know, I know, a strange name for a horse, but that's what she called him. After Tammy was killed, the Kellingtons thought about Tammy every time they saw Snap, and no one at Shady Springs rode him for that very reason. One day, Paul heard about a man who was looking for a horse for his daughter because she had outgrown her pony. Anyway, when Paul delivered Snap to his new owner, the man asked him if he wanted to take his pony as partial payment for the horse. Paul really didn't want the pony, but he knew it hadn't been ridden in quite a while, and there were few horses around to keep it company. He figured if he took her home, at least she'd be around other horses, even if no one at Shady Springs was small enough to ride her, and that's how Snowflake came to live here."

Lillian was glad she knew why Snowflake was at Shady Springs, but she wondered, then asked, "Why can't I ride her instead of riding Honey? I like Honey okay, but she's way too big for me. Sometimes I don't think my legs will stretch that far when I get on her."

Just then, Paul walked in the barn to get something, and Lilly asked, "Papa K, would it be okay if I rode Snowflake today? She's just my size."

He turned to her and smiled. "Snowflake hasn't been ridden in a long time, and you just started riding. I don't know what she'd do, so you'd better not at this time." He saw how disappointed she was, so he said, "But maybe we can fix that. This afternoon, I'll put Brielle on Snowflake and see how she handles. I didn't have Brielle ride her when she got to Shady Springs because I wanted her to start on Honey, like I did you. Then she found Cassidy, and now Cass is the only horse she wants to ride. I thought there was no point in making sure the pony was okay to ride if no one was going to ride her, so I just left her in the pasture with her other horse friends."

Lilly smiled. "*Now* there's a reason. I want to ride her."

Paul smiled down at her. "We'll make that happen, little girl."

Snowflake was a little skittish when Brielle first got on her, but she quickly calmed down. Then it was Lilly's turn to ride. After she was in the saddle, Paul led the little pony around until they were sure she wouldn't act up. He patted her neck. "Good girl. You be nice for Lilly now." Then he let Lilly ride without him holding the bridle. Lilly was proud and thrilled.

When they got back to the barn, she asked, "What kind of horse is Snowflake?"

Paul responded, "She's a Welsh pony. They got their name from Wales, England, which of course is where the Welch people live. The Welsh ponies were used for riding but were often used for plowing fields, pulling wagons, or driving a family to services on Sunday. When coal mining became important to the economy of England, many Welsh ponies were harnessed for use in the mines. When they were brought to Canada and the United States, they adapted easily to our climate."

Brielle started laughing. "I forgot to warn you, Lilly. If you ask Papa K what time it is, he will build you a watch. In other words, if he knows something about a subject, he will tell you *everything* he knows about it, and you don't even have to ask."

Paul pulled back, pretending he was insulted. "So now you're making fun of me?"

Brielle ran over and gave him a big hug. "Nope. I love that about you. It makes you more interesting because you want to share what you know."

He continued, "There is one more thing I haven't shared with you two. Snowflake came with a driving harness and a pony cart."

Lilly jumped up and down and clapped. "Goody! Goody! When can we get a ride in the cart?"

Paul laughed and told them he would try to get Snowflake used to the harness and cart this week, and maybe this weekend they could go for a spin around the ranch.

Bright and early on Saturday morning, the girls tromped down the front steps and found Snowflake waiting in harness with the cart behind her. They were tickled because the harness had bells on it, and the cart was painted red, purple, and gold. "How fun!" they exclaimed as they climbed in the two-seat cart. "What do we do now?"

Paul handed Brielle the reins and said, "Driving is very much like riding, but you must use both hands when you drive. And don't worry. I'll be leading Snowflake at first. Fortunately, she's already trained to harness so she's used to the blinkers on the bridle."

Lilly asked, "What are blinkers and why do they use them?"

Paul explained, "They are pieces of leather sewn on the harness bridle to keep a horse from seeing the cart behind it. You can imagine how scary it might be to a horse to constantly see a cart or wagon following close behind."

Brielle said, "How do I make Snowflake go? I can't give her a little kick or squeeze her with my legs."

"Cluck and say walk, trot, or whatever you want her to do. And gently slap the reins against the top of her back. She'll know what to do."

When Brielle clucked and slapped the reins as instructed, Snowflake moved forward, pulling the cart. Paul led the little mare a minute or two, then let them drive off on their own but hollered after them, "Don't go too fast!"

Lilly was thrilled to be riding in the beautiful cart with jangling bells. All afternoon, the two of them practiced walking, trotting, and stopping on the ranch's roads, but they weren't quite ready to ask Snowflake to gallop, because what if she wouldn't stop?

One late-winter morning, Brenda commented to her husband, "You know, the girls have a birthday coming up in a few weeks, and I want to make it very special for them. I think it's great their birthdays are only two days apart. I've been looking at the calendar, and maybe they'd like to celebrate their birthdays together, because the day in between falls on a Saturday."

Paul liked the idea and said, "Hey, that's something we can discuss if we take them out to the cabin for a sleepover. Lilly's never been there, and Brielle seemed to like it when we went the last time." Brenda agreed.

After dinner, they sat in the living room, all watching the fire that was taking the chill off the room. Paul tapped on the side of his glass to get everyone's attention. "Girls, I have an announcement to make. Tomorrow night is Saturday night, and I think we should go to the cabin for a sleepover."

When Lillian blurted out, "What cabin?" Brenda told her to ask her sister.

She pleaded, "Brie, what cabin are they talking about?"

Brielle answered, "Lilly, you don't have to know everything. Trust us. You'll like it because it will be a great surprise."

They all watched her pout because she wanted to know *now* instead of having to wait.

Mama K said, "It'll be a great adventure for you, and I know you like adventures."

The next afternoon, after the truck was packed, they headed out to the cabin. Brielle commented, "I bet it's pretty out there now but maybe a little nippy."

When they pulled into the long driveway, Lilly shrieked, "I like it! I like it!" and everyone rolled their eyes. She was such a drama queen.

Mama and Papa K fixed dinner while Brielle walked her sister along the shore of Cypress Creek. Fortunately, it was warm enough to eat outside, so everyone gathered at a picnic table on the sleeping porch.

Lilly commented, "This is such a nice surprise. Can we light a fire later?" They all nodded yes. "Outside?" she asked. They all shook their heads no because they knew it would soon be too cool.

After dinner, the four of them gathered around the fireplace as Paul pulled up an extra wingback chair. They all agreed it was cozy and warm.

Brielle asked, "What shall we talk about?"

Paul looked at his wife, then at the girls, and said, "I know what we can talk about." They all looked at him expectantly, so he continued. "Brenda and I have grown to love you both. You know that, right?" He continued without getting an answer. Looking over at Brielle, he said, "You've been here the longest, and I think we've told you many times how we feel about you." Then he looked at Lillian. "You are Brielle's sister, and that means a lot to us. We've found you to be funny, sweet, helpful, and also very lovable. So, here is our proposition. If we can work it out with your mother, would you do us both the honor of letting us adopt you?" The girls sat stunned and silent because it was something they thought was impossible.

Mama K smiled. "Now don't both of you speak at once, and please realize there are a lot of things that have to happen if this is to ever take place. Number one is you have to want us as your legal parents, and number two, your mother and grandmother would have to agree to the adoption." She hastily added before they could speak, "Remember, this is going nowhere if either of you don't like the idea."

Lillian's eyes filled with tears. "But what about my grandmother? I can't leave her because she needs me and would miss me too much."

Brenda quickly spoke up as she reached over and put her hand on Lilly's. "Sweetheart, you would not be giving up your grandmother; you'd just be living here with us and your sister. She could see you whenever she wanted. Of course, we'll talk this over with her as well."

Lillian started sobbing. "But … but she wouldn't want to give me away. She loves me."

Brenda got out of her chair, knelt in front of Lilly, and took her hands. "Sometimes people do what's best for their children or their grandchildren, even though it hurts them. Don't cry about it now because we'll talk with her next week when we go to see her … if that's what you want us to do."

Their attention turned to Brielle. "How about you? Would you like us to be your *forever* parents?"

She was speechless as thoughts sped through her mind. She finally said, "My mom gave me up once because they made her do it. I don't know if she'd do it again, because she might feel like she is abandoning me a second time, and I know she wants me with her when she gets out. I really don't know …" Her voice faded away.

Papa K said, "Girls, I know this is a surprise to you, but even if you decide you don't want us as parents, always remember that we wouldn't have suggested this if we didn't love you." A moment later, Paul jumped up to get the cards. He wanted the girls to think about the possibility of being adopted but didn't want them to make this decision without some thought and discussion among themselves. "Now, what games are we going to play tonight, and who wants to deal first?"

Playing cards had been a good distraction, but when the girls were bundled together in the big bed in the loft, they whispered quietly. Brielle spoke first. "Lilly, were you surprised at what Papa K asked us tonight?"

Lilly answered with a question. "You mean about us being adopted?"

Exasperated, Brielle answered, "Of course that's what I'm talking about. Do you think they meant it?"

"I guess. I've only known them a little while. What do *you* think?"

"I think they really want us. I never thought anyone would want me forever … like a real daughter."

Lilly sat up and looked at her sister in the dim light. "Do you think my abuelita would be mad if I was adopted?"

Brielle answered truthfully, "I don't think so because she likes the Kellingtons and she really can't take care of you anymore."

Lilly posed another question. "Do you think our real mother would be mad at us if we wanted to stay at Shady Springs?"

Brielle answered thoughtfully, "I was just thinking about that. I know she still talks about getting us back when she gets out of prison, but I don't think she'll be out for a long time, and we'll be grown by then."

Lilly lay back down, grabbed her sister's hand, and started crying softly. "I don't want to make anyone mad, but I want to stay here with you. How will I ever be able to tell my grandmother I want to stay here? It would be easier for me to tell your mother … I mean *our* mother … because I've never even met her, but I love my Litta so much, and I don't want to hurt her feelings."

Brielle turned to her in the bed and held her close. "Let's not think about it anymore tonight, because there's nothing we can do about it now. Maybe tomorrow the Kellingtons can tell us what to do if we tell them we want to stay here." As they snuggled together, she said, "Sweet dreams, little sister."

Morning came, and everyone got up, ate breakfast, and went to church. Brenda and Paul thought it strange that no one even mentioned the conversation they had the night before. They wondered if it meant the girls didn't want to be adopted, but just wanted to live with them. Finally, at lunch, Paul asked them if they had thought more about their offer to adopt them.

The girls looked at each other, and Brielle said, "We just don't want to hurt anyone, but yes, we would love to be part of a real family … a forever family."

Brenda let out a sigh of relief. "Girls, would you like for us to talk with your mom and Lilly's grandmother before we decide to go forward with this?"

They answered in unison, "Yes! Would you do that for us? Can you make them understand that we don't want to make them feel bad?"

Paul and Brenda gave them each a hug to reassure them they would *gently* present the adoption offer to the girls' mother and grandmother. Once that was settled, Lilly shouted, "Good! Now let's go ride!" and they did.

The next morning, Paul called the prison and left a message for Anne to call him collect. Twenty minutes later, the phone rang. She sounded frightened when Brenda answered the phone. "Is something wrong with the girls? I got to the phone as quickly as I could. I never get calls, so I thought it must be an emergency."

Brenda reassured her. "No, Anne, nothing's wrong with the girls, but I have a question for you. And please know that I'm not asking this to upset you, but Paul and I would love to adopt the girls, and we are asking for your blessing."

Anne was stunned and responded hotly, "They are *my* babies, and I don't want you to take them from me."

Brenda responded calmly, "We know you are bound to feel that way, but we respectfully ask that you give your permission for the adoption because it would be good for the girls." Anne tried to interrupt, but Brenda continued, "They know you are their mother, and you'll always be their mother, but if we adopt them, they'll have a more normal life and won't be afraid of being sent to another foster home, especially if something happens to one of us. We would legally be a family."

Anne stammered, "I know you are good foster parents, because the girls told me so, but giving away my babies is another thing. What would they think of me, giving them up twice?"

"Listen, Anne. They're afraid if they want to be adopted,

it will hurt you and Lilly's grandmother. Benita cried when I asked her, but she understood she could no longer take care of Lilly because her health is not good and she may die soon. She confessed she was hoping we'd want to adopt Lilly, but selfishly, she wanted to keep her with her as long as possible. She finally told me she would bless the adoption because it would be best for Lilly."

Anne wailed, "But that's different. Benita might die and would not be here to take care of Lillian."

Brenda asked gently, "Are *you* here to take care of those two beautiful little girls?"

"Well no, but I'll be out of here in eight years, and I could take care of them then."

Brenda continued quietly, "But will you be there for them while they are growing up … when they really need love and guidance?"

Anne knew she could not answer yes but said, "I'll have to think and pray about it."

Brenda encouraged her to do so that evening and to give them a call the next morning. She agreed.

Anne had a very rough night, thinking about the finality of an adoption. She desperately wanted her girls with her when she got out of prison, but realized she'd never be able to give them anything like the Kellingtons were giving them now. The girls were both Christians and going to church, they had fun things to do on the ranch, and they had friends that weren't dope heads. Thinking about those advantages stopped her cold. Who would she live with when she got out? Would it be other ex-cons or people who helped ex-cons after they got out of jail? Would she be able to get a job? Send her kids to college? Have a normal life? She told herself she had no answers, but in her heart, she knew she did. She would be poor and struggling, even if she only had to take care of herself. If the girls were adopted by the Kellingtons, they would have lots of advantages, the most important being a stable family life not tainted by a drug, or ex-drug, culture. She didn't know what her future would be, but she knew it would be much more difficult with the two girls.

When Anne was done wrestling with the problem on her own, she took it to God. *Dear Father God, I'm so ashamed of how I've turned out and know I deserve to lose my girls, but they're mine and I love them and want to make it up to them. Every time I think about refusing to let the Kellingtons raise them, I feel guilty and have no peace. What will be best for my girls and best for me? I know You've forgiven me because the Kairos prison ministry ladies made me see that, but I can't undo what I've done, and I guess this is a consequence of my poor choices.*

She heard no answers from God, so she continued, *I believe You placed them with a loving family, but I want them to be with me. Am I being selfish? What will make this pain go away? If I let them go, I would be putting what I desperately want aside so my girls can have a good life. Is that the sacrificial giving the Bible talks about?*

She kept talking to God. *Lord, what I am feeling in my spirit must be from You because as soon as I spoke of unselfish, sacrificial giving, You seemed to lead me to think in that direction. Maybe it means that if I bless the Kellingtons' plans to adopt my girls, I will feel peace. I still don't like giving them away, but You have convinced me that I can show them I love them by releasing them to people who can give them a loving Christian life.*

As soon as she made the decision in her heart, Anne fell into a sound, peaceful sleep, knowing she was going to do the will of God. At ten o'clock the next morning, she called the Kellingtons and told them of her decision and how she now felt peace about giving her blessing. She would sign any paperwork necessary to make the adoption happen.

CHAPTER 15
The Birthday Cookout

Early April in Wimberley was glorious, so it was time for a ride and a picnic down by the river. It wasn't a picnic with a picnic table nearby but the old-fashioned kind where quilts were spread on the ground to keep the morning dew off their clothes. The azalais and bluebonnets surrounding them were in full bloom. Brielle could hardly believe it had been a whole year since she and Papa K had ridden Cassidy into a field to see if she could cut cattle. That's when Brielle learned Cass was a natural cutting horse.

As they were passing around the potato salad and fried chicken, Mama K asked, "What shall we do about your girls' birthdays? They're coming up, you know."

Lilly was ready with an answer. "We can have a cookout at the house and invite Grandma and all our family."

Brielle cautioned her sister, "That would be too expensive."

Lilly continued with a little whine in her voice, "But only my grandmother has been to Shady Springs, and I want my whole family to see where I'm living now."

Papa K smiled and agreed with her. "It would be a great time to meet Lillian's family and to have Benita here again. Her daughters and their families can bring her here to Wimberley for a big party. And you, Brielle, can invite your friends from school too. It should be fun."

Lillian was excited, telling them all about her family, then added, "And maybe they can bring Ready to see me too. I sure do miss my dog."

Papa K again agreed. "It sounds like a good plan. Let's see now. Lillian, your birthday is on April 22, right? And, Brie, yours is on the twentieth. Since the twenty-first is on a Saturday and in between both birthdays, why don't we set that as the party date. That way, we can catch you both at the same time."

All agreed, and Lillian started to plan, driving everyone crazy.

The day of the party was bright and sunny, and cars started arriving around eleven o'clock. When Lilly saw her grandmother in the back of her aunt's car, she ran to open the door. "Oh, Abulieta, I'm so glad you are well enough to come. I saw you last week, but it's not the same as seeing you outside that place you stay now, with all those nurses around. We're going to have such a good time."

Benita was all smiles and let her family help her out of the car and into the house.

Though Brenda had already set up tables using festive tablecloths, Lilly's family got to work draping strings of tiny lights in the trees. The final touch was the hanging of two piñatas so the girls, as the guests of honor, could try whacking them while blindfolded. Lilly could hardly wait until she broke hers and candy and small toys poured out onto the ground.

While they were getting ready to hit the piñatas, Paul began telling the history of this tradition, because, as usual, he had looked it up on the internet. "Everyone believes having piñatas was a Spanish tradition, but history tells us the Chinese had them first. They weren't beautiful like the ones from Mexico but were in the shape of a cow or ox and used for the New Year celebrations, hoping the gods would bring a favorable climate for the coming growing season. After the piñatas were broken, the remains were burned and the ashes kept for good luck. Later, in Spain, they were used in the Christian celebration of Lent. The European piñata tradition was brought to Mexico in the sixteenth century; however, there was a similar tradition in Mesoamerica already …"

His voice trailed off because no one was paying attention to him. They were more interested in watching the girls get ready with their big sticks, wanting the piñatas to be broken so they could scoop up candy and toys. He really didn't blame them because he knew they were having fun.

Paul stood with his arm around Brenda's shoulder, and just before they cut the birthday cake, he said, "Quiet, everyone. I have an announcement to make." After the music was turned down and everyone looked his way, he continued, "I want to announce that I have spoken with both Brielle and Lillian's mother, as well as her grandmother, and all agree that we should adopt Brielle and Lillian."

This was the first time the girls had heard the adoption was going forward. They hugged each other, smiling and crying at the same time. Their friends and family cheered and rushed in to congratulate them.

Brielle spoke for both herself and her sister. "I'm speechless … well almost, because I *am* talking right now, but this is such a happy day for us. We never believed we would ever have a forever family like other kids." She looked over at Benita. "We both thank you from the bottom of our hearts because we knew the Kellingtons would not adopt us without agreement from everyone." She looked down at her sister, who was smiling and nodding enthusiastically. "What a gift of love this is, and we know it."

Paul asked for their attention again. "I almost forgot. We have one more special gift for Lillian. She is now the proud owner of Snowflake." He looked over at her and could see the shock on her face.

Lilly's hand went up to her mouth in surprise. She couldn't believe they could be that generous. She now owned Snowflake— the pony she had grown to love so much! She turned to Brielle, gave her a quick hug, and called for her dog, Ready. Two men ran to the barn to tell Snowflake the good news.

Lilly's grandmother was smiling but had watched enough of the celebration for now, so she didn't object when she was gently helped inside and settled in a bed. As Brenda drew a light coverlet up over her, she said, "Don't worry, Benita. You can rest here but still hear everyone outside. I'll be in to check on you, so don't worry about a thing." She leaned down and kissed her on the forehead.

The party was still going strong when the sun went down. The lights in the trees were twinkling, and the mariachi CDs Lilly's family had brought continued to play. It was a wonderful birthday celebration, and the girls loved it because they were surrounded by both family and friends.

About eight o'clock, everyone started packing up because the children were tired and getting cranky. All hugged and thanked the Kellingtons for the opportunity to see where Lillian now lived and to celebrate her sixth birthday and upcoming adoption. They woke Benita up, and Paul carried her to the car after she gave Lilly a birthday kiss. Lilly saw tears in her eyes.

"Goodbye, my chiquita. I hope you had a wonderful birthday. Remember, I gave my permission for the Kellingtons to adopt you *because* I love you, *not* because I don't want to take care of you any longer. I can see they love you very much."

Lillian called her grandmother every evening after dinner but was not sure she was getting better. The calls became shorter and shorter as the weeks went on because Benita was often in the hospital and so weak she couldn't talk long. One evening, a nurse called and told Brenda that Lillian's grandmother was in the hospital again, and Lilly needed to come see her very soon. Lilly was stricken with fear when she heard and sobbed, "What if she dies?"

Loving arms wrapped around her and drew her up into a soft, warm lap. Brenda held her close and stroked her hair as she reassured her they would leave for San Antonio first thing in the morning. Before Lilly went to bed, she asked Brielle if she would sleep in her bed with her because she was afraid she would have sad dreams about her grandmother. Brielle said she would, and they snuggled up together, with Brie softly singing a lullaby to help her little sister relax and drift off to sleep.

At seven o'clock the next morning, Mama K looked in Brielle's room to wake her for breakfast, but she wasn't there. Brenda knew where to look next. She had forgotten Brielle was sleeping with her sister. When she opened Lilly's bedroom door, she could see two figures wrapped up in a blanket on the bed. She smiled because she knew love when she saw it. After gently shaking Brielle's toes, she whispered, "Wake up, sleepyhead. We've got things to do today. Remember, Lilly's going to need your support today."

Both girls sat up, stretched, then got out of bed and plodded to their bathroom. They liked sharing a bath between them because that way, if they wanted to visit each other at night, they wouldn't have to go into the hall. They could just cut through the bathroom.

It took Lilly a minute to remember where they were going that morning ... to San Antonio to visit her grandma! She said a quick prayer. *Dear God, make my abuelita get well because I love her so much. Amen.*

Benita was lying very still when they arrived. When Lilly

spoke, she saw a slight smile form on her grandmother's lips, but there was no other movement. She took her hand and said, "Abuelita, if you can hear me, squeeze my hand. I just want to know you understand what I'm telling you." She felt a very weak squeeze. "Please know that I love you and want you to get better, but if you are in pain and want to go to Jesus, I want you to go. It won't hurt my feelings, because even though I'm only six, I understand," Again, there was another squeeze.

They stayed a few hours more, but the nurse said Benita was sleeping and would probably not wake up for hours, if ever, which made Lilly cry. After a few minutes of discussion, they decided to go back to Wimberley. In the car, she cried silently, then announced, "My Litta will not wake up again, but she knows I love her and she can go on. In heaven, she'll be well, and that's what I want … for her to be well again." She wiped her tears on her sleeve, then said, "I know I'll see her again because we are both God's children." With that, she dried her face, smiled, then murmured a prayer, "Thank you, Jesus, for giving us a way to let the people we love go to live with You. Amen."

Brenda was quiet the rest of the ride home while she thought about what this small but wise six-year-old had said and how calmly she was accepting the probable death of her grandmother. If only adults could let people they love go on to a better place instead of holding on. She wanted to remember Lilly's example and try to act as unselfishly if faced with the upcoming death of someone she loved.

EPILOGUE

Benita died, but Lillian and her family chose to celebrate her life instead of being sad. The wake and funeral were events of peace and joy as they remembered the positive things about her life. Paul hesitated to use the word *refreshing*, but that is what it became—a wonderful hallelujah day celebrating the passage of a godly woman into the arms of Jesus.

Questions for Discussion

1. Discuss how Brielle felt when she arrived at Shady Springs Ranch and why. Why did she believe her feelings were justified? Have you made assumptions about people that have turned out to be wrong? Describe them.

2. Discuss four specific things that made Brielle change her mind about the Kellingtons.

3. Discuss how Brielle related the Kellingtons' love of rescuing horses to her situation. What similarities did you find between the two?

4. How has your treatment of people of different backgrounds made others view your life as a Christian?

If you enjoyed this book, you might also enjoy
Carolina Dream

Below is an excerpt:

Chapter 1

"Mackenzie, will you please be a sweetheart and go out and get the mail? I'm busy fixing lunch, and I know you're hungry."

She answered, "Yes, Papa," as she passed through their small kitchen. Minutes later, she came in with a big stack and dumped it on the kitchen table. "It seems we get more mail every day."

He shook his head as he sliced a big tomato. "It's a shame someone has to die before friends will send cards or write. In the old days—"

"I know, I know, Papa. People used to write letters to each other before we had email."

He laughed. "You always seem to know what I'm going to say."

"That's because you say the same thing every time I bring in the mail."

He smiled and shook his head. "Yes, I guess I do." He looked over at the stack of mail, washed and dried his hands, then sat down at the table. "Let's see who has blessed us with cards today."

He slowly shuffled through the stack, smiling when he found a letter from someone they hadn't heard from in a long time. Suddenly, he stopped and examined it more closely. *This can't be. This one's from my papa. I haven't spoken to him for almost fifteen years.*

Mackenzie noticed a strange look on her father's face. "What's the matter, Papa?"

He looked up and smiled. "It's nothing, sweetheart. It's just a letter from your grandfather."

She snorted. "From the one I've never talked to or met?"

"Now, Mackenzie, that's no way to talk. He was nice enough to send us a letter."

"Papa, you never told me why you and your family are not close—or why you left Spain."

He looked sad. "It's a tragic story, my little one, but one I probably need to tell you. After I finish fixing your lunch, we can go sit on the porch and talk."

She stomped her foot. "No! I want to hear it now. You always told me you left Spain because you wanted to find a job in America, but I know that's not the whole story, and it's something I've always wanted to know."

He wiped his hands on a dish towel and asked her to sit down. "Mackenzie, I told you our love story, and it was the truth, because I would never lie to you. As you know, your mother and I met on a beautiful sunny day, at a horse show in Spain." He smiled. "We fell in love, and stayed in love, because of our love for horses. I wanted to come to America and work at a big horse farm, so I answered ads in the paper. Finally, one showed an interest. I guess they liked that I'd been raised around horses on a very well-known horse farm near Granada, Spain. They figured I had the experience they needed, so they offered me a job right here on Sunrise Farm ... the farm where we live now."

"Papa, I know all this. Tell me something I *don't* know." Then she thought of another question. "By the way, why did you take a job at a farm in Camden, South Carolina? There are others you might have chosen."

"To tell you the truth, Mac, it was the only one that answered my application. The others ignored it. So, I guess you can say it was God that led us here, and I've not regretted it for a second."

She smiled and nodded. "Now, tell me the rest of the story, the part I don't know."

He frowned but had laughter in his eyes. "Be patient, Mackenzie. I'm getting to it." He took a sip of water, then continued. "As I've said many times before, your mom and I fell in love in Spain, and we were married there. What you don't know is my parents disliked your mother intensely. In fact, they hated her."

His daughter was shocked. "Why? She was the nicest person I've ever known. How could they hate her?"

"They didn't like your mother because she was not Catholic. Back then, Catholics could not marry anyone who was not Catholic, because they'd be excommunicated if they did. Excommunicated means they would be thrown out of the church. My parents were very old-fashioned and thought it was the worst thing that could ever happen to a family. They thought marrying outside the Catholic Church meant their son or daughter would go to hell when they died."

"Wow, that's pretty drastic. So, you left because they didn't like Mom?"

"I left because they told me they didn't want to ever see me again ... that I was dead to them because of what I had done."

Mackenzie was alarmed. "Papa, how could they do that? They were your parents! They were supposed to love you no matter what!"

He returned his attention to the letter. "Since this letter is in Spanish, I'll translate it for you as I read. My father started out with 'Dear Son,' which surprised me since he'd basically disowned me." He continued reading, "'I know you write to your brother, Angelo, and he told me your wife died recently. I offer you my prayers and have been lighting candles in hopes you find peace with your loss. Your mother died two years ago, so I know how you must feel. My biggest regret in life is that I never contacted you and never got to meet my granddaughter, but I know her name is Mackenzie. Angelo showed me pictures of her each time you sent them, and she's beautiful. Give her a hug from me, and tell her I have loved her in my heart since the time she was first born. She's my only grandchild. I am very sick and will not be around much longer, but I want to give you a gift, in hopes you'll forgive this old man his stupid, stubborn ways.'" Miguel read further but silently: *Don't read this part to your daughter, but I am sending you something I love, in hopes you will think of me sometimes. Your gift will arrive in about two weeks … and bring a horse trailer with you when you go to pick it up. You'll get another letter from me when it is delivered.* Her dad started reading aloud again. "'I'm thinking of you. Te amo tanto mucho. Su padre.'"

"Papa, what does the Spanish part mean?"

He looked over at her with tears in his eyes. "It means I love you very much. Your father."

She said, "Aww, how sweet. It's about time he told you he loved you." Then she asked, "What do you think he's sending you?"

"Whatever it is, Mac, I'll treasure it because it'll be from my papa."

"How can you forgive him for driving you and Mom from their lives?"

"God tells us to forgive and helps us do it. It hurt a lot when it first happened, but the pain gradually went away when we had you and a wonderful life here with the horses. Now, I just feel bad that he missed out on loving you and seeing you grow up. So, the loss is really his."

She remarked hotly, "What about me? I lost out too. I never even got to meet him!"

"Punkin, your loss is part of the tragedy, because he loved horses like we do, and you would've been crazy about him. But yes, your loss was terrible as well, because you never got to know each other."

"Why does God tell us to forgive people who hurt us like that? It's not what we feel like doing."

"When we forgive someone, we're being obedient to what the Bible tells us to do. God knows forgiving someone helps us to release anger we sometimes hold inside, because it frees us up to focus on other things, like loving each other and our precious horses."

Chapter 2

Knowing a gift was coming from her grandfather was driving Mackenzie crazy, which meant she was driving her father crazy. "Papa, what on earth could take so long to get from Spain to South Carolina? If you know what it is, tell me. Why won't you tell me? I'm your daughter. Will I like it? Don't be so mean. I want to know." Her dad told her he should have known better than to tell her anything about the gift because he knew she would keep pestering him to tell her what it was.

Two weeks later, they got a call requesting they pick up a large shipment at the Charleston Port Authority. Mackenzie wondered what kind of gift would take two weeks to get from Spain to South Carolina. She was even more perplexed when her dad hitched a horse trailer to his truck. She commented, "It must be a pretty big gift to need a trailer to haul it home." Her dad smiled but said nothing.

Two hours later, they arrived at the Charleston port, and a guard directed them to the live freight section. Mackenzie looked around, wondering why the gift would come by ship. Suddenly, a door opened, and a dock worker led a beautiful light grey mare to where they were standing. Then he carefully read from the document in his hand. "Are you Miguel Perez? If so, please sign this invoice to certify your shipment was delivered."

Her dad answered yes, then signed without taking his eyes

off the horse. He was accustomed to seeing beautiful horses on Sunrise Farm, but this one took his breath away. She was gorgeous. He was then handed a thick envelope, which he quickly opened and started reading. It was another letter from his father. This time he read it out loud, "'Miguel, I want to introduce you to Sueño Ibérico, or as you would say, Iberian Dream. Her papers are in order and included in this envelope. I've also taken the liberty of enclosing documents certifying this beautiful mare was bred to my best stud, Sueño de Plata, which, as you know, means Silver Dream. She is due to foal next April. My wish is that Mackenzie be given this foal from her grandfather, with his love, and that you two may ride these horses together for many years to come.'" Tear flowed down her father's cheeks as he read. Hearing from his dad was emotional, but he continued reading to his daughter.

Mackenzie's eyes opened wide when the letter said the mare was to have a foal, and when it was born, it was to be given to her. She started crying as well. She couldn't believe she would soon have a horse of her own! She'd always been able to ride some of the horses at Sunrise, but this was different. This would be her *own* horse—for her to love, train, and ride. Her tears came so fast she started hiccupping, making the mare toss her head and quickly back up. This made her started laughing, and her dad smiled.

When they got home, Dream was led to a freshly cleaned stall, where she nibbled the hay, then began loudly sucking water from her bucket. She was thirsty from her long trip.

Her dad made sure all the other horses at Sunrise were comfortable and taken care of, but he kept checking on the mare, still not believing she was there and his.

The next day, Mackenzie and her dad took Dream out of her stall to get a better look at her. She was a beautiful dappled grey. The filly pranced as he led her around the paddock, her long mane and tail shimmering in the sunlight.

When he finally saddled her, he rode out to the pasture where Dream could stretch her legs after the long trip. He was surprised when the grooms at Sunrise left the stables to watch. They clapped and whistled as he put her through her paces. It made him proud of his horse but worried him because he didn't want his boss thinking he was trying to draw attention away from the Sunrise horses.

After their short ride, he took Dream back to her stall. While brushing her, he muttered under his breath, "Thoroughbreds are bred to go fast, and my horse was not. They aren't in competition with each other at all."

The next day, Sunrise's owner, Martin Collins, stopped by to see the new addition, and they talked. "Miguel, so this is the horse your father said he was sending? She's not a Thoroughbred, like most of the horses here, but she's a beauty. Didn't you say her name is Iberian Dream?"

"Yes, sir. She's an Andalusian and more beautiful than I expected. She also has a PRE before her registered name, which stands for Pura Raza Espanola. That certifies she's a horse of the pure Spanish breed. It may not mean much here in the United States, where there aren't many Andalusians, but it does in Spain and to the Andalusian horse community around the world."

"So, it's true, your dad is a big-time horse breeder in Spain? I know you're good with horses, but I wondered if what your application for employment said was true."

"Yes, sir, but not a breeder like you, Mr. Collins. I know raising Thoroughbreds is a *really* big deal here in the States." That made his boss smile.

He patted Miguel on the back. "Glad we have room for her with us. That might change in the future, but for now, she's very welcome."

Miguel was pleased to get compliments on his new mare but

a little uneasy when Mr. Collins implied they might not always have room for Dream at Sunrise Farms. When he got home, he was careful not to share his concerns with Mackenzie because it would worry her.

ABOUR THE AUTHOR

Connie Squiers is a graduate of Regent University School of Law in Virginia Beach and in 2004 moved to Tulsa, Oklahoma to live near her sister. Growing up, she remembers the times she spent with her horse crazy girlfriends and reading many, many books about horses. She has used those experiences, and those as a mother, to craft her stories. Always a lover of horses, she decided she could write books that were about horses, were appealing to young people, and would incorporate the tenets of her faith. Her goal has been to show youngsters, and adults alike, that Jesus could, and should, be an integral part of their lives.. She continues to write, and her goal is to make youngsters aware that Jesus can be their best friend.

Printed in the United States
By Bookmasters